Murder in Monaco

A LOTTIE SPRIGG MYSTERY BOOK 4

MARTHA BOND

ISBN 978-1-7396766-6-7

marthabond.com

Lottie Sprigg Travels Mystery Series

~

Murder in Venice
Murder in Paris
Murder in Cairo
Murder in Monaco
Murder in Vienna

Murder in Monaco

Chapter One

'SHE'S LATE,' said Gabriel Boyer, checking his watch. 'Do you think she's going to turn up?'

'I hope so,' replied Maurice Brunelle. 'We can't do this without her.'

Gabriel felt impatient to get out of the coffee shop and have a look around. This was his first visit to Monaco, and he wanted to see the expensive shops, flashy motor cars and large boats in the harbour. Although he was here on business, he hoped he'd have some time for sight-seeing, too. Perhaps a quick look at the Prince's Palace? And the famous casino. Would he get a chance to go inside?

He drummed his fingers on the table, wondering what to say next. Brunelle was dull company. He was the senior of the two and set in his ways. Brunelle wasn't the sort to listen to modern ideas from a junior detective like Gabriel.

'Perhaps we should order another coffee,' suggested the younger man.

'Are you joking? We've already spent half our daily budget, and it isn't even lunchtime yet.'

'I can't believe we only get five francs a day for expenses. Don't they know how much a cup of coffee costs in Monaco?'

'No. They only know how much it costs in Marseille.'

'They should adjust the amount according to where we are.'

'That would make sense, Boyer. And the department is not known for making decisions based on sense.'

Gabriel sighed and dreamed of being a rich actor or businessman who was visiting Monaco for pleasure. Staying in the largest suite at the finest hotel and strolling about the place with a glamorous lady on his arm. Talking of which...

A beautiful, long-limbed woman was now strolling into the cafe. She wore a fur over her shoulders, an amethyst purple jacket and a low-waisted silk dress. Her cloche hat was garnished with a single lily and long beaded necklaces draped from her neck. She headed directly for the two gentlemen, her head held high.

Gabriel gulped. Beautiful women left him tongue-tied.

Maurice got to his feet and Gabriel did the same.

'Madame Rochefort,' said Maurice. 'It's a pleasure to meet you.'

She dropped her cream leather handbag onto the table, sat down, crossed her legs and pursed her red rosebud lips.

The two detectives also sat. 'May I ask, madame,' said Maurice. 'How you knew it was us?'

'Because you look like policemen.' She spoke in a fast Parisian accent.

'But how? We're wearing plain clothes.'

'They look like clothes policemen would wear. And you act like policemen. You even smell like policemen.' Her button nose gave a disparaging twitch. 'You need to do more to blend in.'

Gabriel wondered how he was going to blend in on a budget of only five francs a day.

'I see. Well, we shall see what we can do. I'm Maurice Brunelle and this is my deputy, Gabriel Boyer. We are from the Marseille police department and we've been speaking with our colleagues in Paris who I understand you've been in discussions with.'

'Good. So you've been fully briefed.'

'Yes.'

Gabriel felt a pang of worry. He wasn't sure whether they'd been fully briefed or not. He watched Madame Rochefort as she placed a long, elegant cigarette into a silver holder.

'Allow me, madame.' Maurice held out his lighter and Gabriel couldn't pull his gaze away from Madame Rochefort as she placed the shiny holder between her red lips and dipped the tip of her cigarette into the flame. Then her wide, dark eyes turned to him and he quickly glanced away.

'So how long have you been watching Albertini for?' she asked.

Philippe Albertini was a notorious criminal from Marseille. They'd arrested plenty of his associates, but they never managed to collar him.

'I've been watching him for three years,' said Maurice.

'And you've still not caught him?'

'Well... sometimes it's better to carry out surveillance first.'

'For three years?'

'The surveillance has led us to many criminals during that time.'

'And all the while, Albertini continues to bribe, blackmail, racketeer and smuggle opium from Turkey?'

'He won't be doing it for much longer, Madame Rochefort.'

'Good. So now you need me to tell you where he's meeting my husband. Is that right?'

'Yes please.'

'They are meeting in the casino this evening.'

'Excellent. Thank you.'

'So you will arrest him then?'

'No.'

'No?'

'We shall continue with our surveillance.'

'What? Why can't you just arrest him this evening?'

'Our departmental orders are to watch him and then make the arrest once we are given approval from higher up.'

Madame Rochefort gave a laugh. 'The police have a strange way of doing things. Can you assure me Albertini will be arrested within the next few days?'

'He will be, madame.'

'Good. And my husband? It's extremely important that he's arrested, too.'

'Yes he will be, madame.'

'And me? In return for my cooperation, I shall have the freedom to do whatever I like after this?'

'Yes, madame.'

She smiled broadly and Gabriel was enchanted by the dimples in her cheeks.

'Thank you, Monsieur Brunelle,' she said. 'I'm looking forward to this very much.'

Chapter Two

THE SUN GLISTENED on the Mediterranean Sea as Lottie and her corgi, Rosie, strolled along the clifftop terraces behind Monte Carlo's famous casino. The terraces were edged with stone balustrades, ornate lampposts and palm trees. From this vantage point, Lottie could see the boats in the harbour and the town dazzling white in the sun as it hugged the land between the sea and the mountains. Beyond the harbour rose a rocky headland - the Rock of Monaco - where the Prince's Palace sat behind fortified walls.

Lottie breathed in the warm, fresh air. The climate here was refreshing after the hot, dusty streets of Cairo. She and her employer, Mrs Moore, had arrived in Monaco the previous evening. They'd travelled here with a man who Mrs Moore was hoping to marry, Prince Manfred of Bavaria. He and his entourage were being hosted by the Prince of Monaco in his palace. Apparently, the two princes were good friends.

'Let's find somewhere nice to sit in the sun,' Lottie said to Rosie. They walked down a flight of steps to a lower terrace. Below them, and closer to the sea, was a railway station. A train was pulling out of it, puffing clouds of steam into the air.

Walking along the terrace, they found an empty bench, but Rosie was more interested in a small black bundle lying beneath it.

'What is it?' asked Lottie, as the dog sniffed at it. She bent down to look and realised it was a jacket. Pulling it out, she gave it a shake and saw it was a smart gentleman's dinner jacket. It no doubt belonged to someone who'd sat on the bench the previous evening, perhaps recovering from an unlucky night at the casino tables.

Lottie sat on the bench and looked in the jacket pockets, hoping something would identify the owner. She found an empty cigar case, a lighter, some centime coins and an empty wallet.

'There's no name anywhere,' she said to Rosie. The dog sniffed at the leg of the bench, then lay down in a patch of shade. Lottie wondered how she could reunite the jacket with its owner. She imagined he was in a hotel nearby, sleeping off the previous evening. Or perhaps he'd hopped onto a train and left Monaco altogether.

'I suppose the best we can do is take this to the casino and maybe the person who owns it might return there in the hope someone's handed it in. He might come back to this bench, but I think the jacket will be safer in the casino. It would be a shame if someone stole it.'

The jacket had a red silk lining and Lottie noticed an inside pocket which she hadn't yet looked in. She put her hand in and pulled out a crumpled note.

I warned you but you didn't listen, now ~~your~~ you're for it.

It took Lottie a moment to realise how threatening the words were. 'How horrible!' she said to Rosie. 'I suppose we should be impressed that he or she corrected their grammar. But why write something so nasty?'

The note had been written on headed paper from the

Hôtel Hermitage Monte-Carlo. It had been crumpled up and pushed into the pocket, as if hurriedly placed there.

Lottie now felt intrigued to find out who the owner of the jacket was. Were they in danger? Had something unfortunate already happened to them? How long had the note been there? Was it from the previous night or had it been sitting in the pocket for longer?

The note was written in English and they were in a French-speaking country. Did that mean the owner of the jacket was English? And the author of the note?

Although the note was worrying, there was little Lottie could do about it. 'All we can do is take this to the casino and hope it gets returned to its rightful owner. Come on, Rosie.'

They climbed the steps again and made their way up to the casino. It was an attractive, cream building decorated with carved stone and two ornate domed towers. It overlooked the Place du Casino, a square edged with palm trees. One side of the square was filled with tables from the Cafe de Paris while another side was occupied by the hotel Lottie and Mrs Moore were staying at - the Hôtel de Paris.

Lottie and Rosie made their way past the shiny motor cars parked outside the casino and climbed the steps. A decorative wrought iron portico stretched over their heads and a doorman in blue and red livery watched them approach. He was no doubt wondering what a young woman in a plain cotton sundress and her dog were doing at such an exclusive establishment. He had narrow eyes and a prominent chin.

Lottie held out the jacket to him and spoke in French. She'd learnt the language at her orphanage, courtesy of Miss Beaufort the French schoolmistress.

'I found this jacket under a bench on the terrace behind the casino,' she said. 'I think it was probably left there by someone who was here last night. I've checked the pockets, but I can't find out who it belongs to.' She decided not to mention the threatening note. If the doorman decided to look through the pockets himself, then he would soon discover it and then it would be up to him what he made of it. And that depended on how good his comprehension of English was.

'Thank you.' He took the jacket from her. 'It was left under a bench?'

'Yes. I suppose someone took it off and forgot about it.'

'He may have heard a train arrive and ran for it, forgetting all about his jacket. The train station is conveniently located for people who've had a difficult night here.' He smiled. 'They can get away quickly.'

Lottie thanked him and went on her way, trying to push thoughts of the threatening note from her mind. Its contents had cast a cloud on a bright and beautiful day.

Chapter Three

BACK AT THE HOTEL, Lottie found Mrs Moore on her balcony, enjoying a cup of coffee at a little table. She wore her blue silk robe with a Japanese print on it.

'Lottie!' she greeted her with a beam on her face. 'Have you been out for a walk already? I'm not surprised. It's beautiful out there, isn't it?' She gestured at the blue expanse of the twinkling Mediterranean. 'I adore this room!' she said. 'Isn't the view wonderful?' She picked up her lorgnette and took in the panorama. 'And over there, on that headland, is where my prince is staying! I shouldn't call him my prince, that doesn't sound right, does it? But I can't help myself. I wonder when I shall see him next? I suppose he would like a bit of time to catch up with his old friend, the Prince of Monaco, but hopefully he'll call on me soon. He knows we're staying at the Hôtel de Paris and he said he'd be in touch, so hopefully I'll receive a message imminently. Wouldn't it be wonderful if we received an invitation to the palace?'

'It would be something.' Lottie sat at the table and peered over the balcony railings. Below them was a road, then a path along the clifftop, where a group of ladies paraded with parasols and a couple of gentlemen chatted beneath the shade of a palm tree.

'It's all very refined and genteel, isn't it?' said Mrs Moore. 'I must say, I get a bit confused about how this country is set up. Prince Manfred's interpreter, Boris, explained it to us on the boat over here, didn't he? But I'm afraid I struggled to fully grasp it. Although we're in France, we're actually in another country, aren't we? The principality of Monaco.'

'Boris said the Grimaldi family took control of the territory in the 13th century and they've been in charge ever since,' said Lottie. 'A treaty was signed in 1861 which established Monaco as a protectorate of the French Empire.'

'Golly, Lottie. How do you remember everything he told us? You have a wonderful ability to retain information. I know he explained to us the difference between Monte Carlo and Monaco, but I don't think I can remember that either.'

'Monaco is divided into four districts and Monte Carlo is one of them. It's where we are now, the district around the casino.'

'Well remembered, Lottie.'

'And Prince Manfred is in Monaco-Ville which is the old city.'

'The bit on the rock. I understand.'

'Monaco is smaller than Central Park.'

'Now I remember that fact. A country smaller than a park! Quite unbelievable. And I'll certainly never set foot in Central Park again.'

'Why not?'

'When I was a child, my sister and I had a carriage ride there. But something spooked the horse, and it ran off, out of control!'

'Oh no, did the carriage crash?'

'Thankfully not. The horse calmed down in the end. But not before taking me and my sister on a death-defying tour of the place! Never again. Just the mention of Central Park brings it all back. Let's talk about something else.'

Lottie told her about the jacket she'd found and the note in its pocket. 'I hope the jacket gets returned to its owner,' she added.

'That note doesn't sound very nice at all. I find gambling brings out the worst in people, and that's why I'm determined to stay away from the casino. No good can ever come of it. Even when people win lots of money, they can't help going back again only to lose it all. You can never make money from gambling. It's rigged. The house always wins.'

Lottie wasn't so sure that the threatening note had anything to do with gambling. 'I wonder why someone would even write a note like that,' she said.

'My advice is to forget about it, Lottie. It may even have been a joke. A bit of a strange joke, I grant you that. But a joke all the same. You can't get involved with other people's lives. It's for the chap who owns the jacket to sort out. Good golly, what's that noise?'

The growl of an engine grew louder as a vehicle roared up the road from the harbour. They peered over the balcony to see a sporty red motor car passing by. Its engine switched to a deeper rumble as the car slowed for the corner between the casino and the hotel. Then the engine spluttered and popped and they heard another roar as it picked up speed again in the Place du Casino.

'What a menace!' exclaimed Mrs Moore. 'Aren't some people selfish in the way they drive about? Everyone else is having a pleasant quiet morning and some miscreant in a motor car ruins it all by zooming through with no cares at all!'

LATER THAT MORNING, Lottie, Mrs Moore and Rosie sauntered along the harbour where immaculate yachts and pleasure boats bobbed on the gentle waves. They encountered fashionable people with well-groomed dogs and exchanged pleasantries about their animals and the weather.

'It's a bit like being in Paris again, isn't it, Lottie? Only by the sea.'

As they reached the end of the harbour, the wooded slopes of the Rock of Monaco rose above them. Mrs Moore peered up at the fortified walls at the top. 'That's where Prince Manfred is. Shall we go up there?'

'It looks like a long walk,' said Lottie.

'There's a pathway, look, you can see it zig-zagging across.'

'But it still looks like a long walk.' Lottie felt wary of a hilly climb while the sun was high in the midday sky.

'Well, I don't know about you, Lottie, but I have lots of energy today. Even though I'm more than twice your age!' Mrs Moore laughed. 'Come along. And if we're lucky, Prince Manfred will let us into the Prince's Palace at the top.'

Lottie looked down at her plain dress. 'But I don't have the right outfit for the Prince's Palace!'

'I'm sure they won't mind.'

The first section of the climb took them on a pleasant stroll through woodland. Rosie enjoyed the shade and sniffed among the plants and tree trunks. Mrs Moore was in a good mood, humming a merry tune and pointing out the view as they glimpsed it between the trees.

The section ended at a sharp turn, which led to the next uphill path. Mrs Moore's breathing was a little heavier than usual, but she was showing no signs of slowing. Lottie imagined she was feeling warm in her heavy Edwardian skirts and high-necked blouse.

After another sharp bend, the path climbed up out of the woodland and reached the base of the fortress walls. There was no shade now, and Lottie felt tired. Mrs Moore was breathing too heavily to talk. Only Rosie seemed unaffected, trotting ahead and investigating every scent she could find.

As they came to another bend, Mrs Moore rested on the wall to catch her breath. 'Golly, this is turning out to be further than I thought.' She looked up at the walls. 'How much longer?'

'We can stop here and admire the view for a moment.'

'What a good idea.'

They could see across the harbour to the other headland, where the buildings lined the road which ran up the hill and curved in between the hotel and the casino.

'You can see our hotel from here,' said Lottie.

'Can you?'

'In fact, your room is probably one of those windows.'

'Is it?'

Mrs Moore didn't seem enormously interested.

Beyond the headland, the coastline receded into the distance in a series of grey-blue headlands growing paler between the aquamarine sea and sky. Inland rose steep mountains. They were rocky and sparsely covered with green. Boris, Prince Manfred's interpreter, had informed Lottie and Mrs Moore that these were the Maritime Alps, the southern part of the Alpine region.

A bird chirruped from the trees below them and the sun was warm on Lottie's face. It was a beautiful location.

She turned to look up at the walls looming over them. 'I think we're nearly there.'

'We'd better be. It would be awfully embarrassing if I didn't make it.'

'You'll make it, Mrs Moore, we just need to walk slowly.'

But after the next stretch, Mrs Moore's face was wet with perspiration. 'I'm not going to make it. Your nineteen-year-old legs have beaten my fifty-year-old ones.'

'Yes you will make it, you've come this far. We're nearly there.'

'You and Rosie go on and fetch Prince Manfred for me,' she puffed. 'Perhaps he can bring me out a nice cold glass of lemonade?'

Lottie didn't fancy calling at the palace and asking for lemonade for her employer. 'Come on Mrs Moore, you can do it.'

'I can't.'

'You can!'

'I can't!'

'One last push!'

'You'll have to drag me up the last bit, then.'

Mrs Moore held out her hand and Lottie pulled her up the very last section of path which ended between the tall stone walls.

'Shade!' Mrs Moore leant against the cool stone, catching her breath. After a few minutes, she was ready to walk on. 'Thank you, Lottie, for getting me up here. I couldn't have done it without you.'

'I'm sure you could have.'

'It's well fortified up here, isn't it? No wonder the same family has been in charge for over 700 years. No one could get at them on this impenetrable rock!'

They passed through another gateway before ascending some steps and eventually emerging in a wide, open plaza. Stretched along one side of it was the Prince's Palace. It was an odd mix of styles, suggesting it had been added to over the years. It had rows of elegant arched windows, a pinky-cream facade and sections which looked like a castle with crenelated towers and narrow windows.

On the opposite side of the plaza, pastel-coloured buildings housed a cafe and a shop. Behind them was a wall which overlooked the harbour, giving the best view of Monaco they had seen yet. Some tourists mingled in the plaza and admired the view.

'So this is where Prince Manfred is staying,' said Mrs Moore. Her breathing was still a little laboured. 'Do you think we can call on him?'

Lottie eyed the guards in navy and red uniform standing sentry. They didn't look particularly welcoming. 'I'm not sure,' she said. 'It looks like the sort of place you visit by appointment.'

'But we're friends of the prince, aren't we? I know what you mean, though, Lottie. It all looks rather formal and officious. I think we'll have to settle for a drink at this cafe instead. I wonder what the prince is doing in there?'

Chapter Four

THE DESCENT DOWN the Rock of Monaco was easier than the climb. But Lottie and Mrs Moore felt exhausted as they made their way up from the harbour to the hotel. Rosie lagged behind them, so Lottie picked her up and carried her.

'Well, look at that,' said Mrs Moore, during one of her many pauses for breath. 'Someone's driven into the wall here.'

A section of the neat balustrade wall, which separated the path from the cliff face, lay in broken pieces of rubble.

'I hope nobody went over into the sea,' continued Mrs Moore. 'Was the wall like that when we passed it earlier?'

'I think so.'

'I didn't notice it. Goodness me, I'm so tired I think I might sleep all day tomorrow. For once, I'm hoping Prince Manfred doesn't get in touch about doing something.'

AFTER AN AFTERNOON REST, Mrs Moore was a little more recovered and Lottie sensed she was disappointed she'd heard nothing yet from Prince Manfred.

Dinner that evening began as a quiet affair. The hotel

restaurant overlooked the Place du Casino and, from their table by the window, Lottie and Mrs Moore had a good view of people coming and going.

'This is a delightful spot to be nosy from, isn't it, Lottie? We can see right across the square to the Cafe de Paris.'

They had just finished their lobster bisque when the window vibrated with the throb of a motor car engine. A moment later, they watched the bright red sports car pull up.

'There's that noisy motor car again, Lottie!'

They watched as a squat figure climbed out of the car. The person was dressed in motoring overalls, a hat which came down over their ears and thick-lensed driving goggles.

'He's not one of the guests, is he?' said Mrs Moore as the figure made their way to the door of the hotel. 'Can that inconsiderate motorist really be one of the guests here? I'm surprised they don't tell him off for driving about like that!'

A moment later, the driver in overalls strode into the restaurant.

'You'd think he could have changed for dinner, Lottie!' hissed Mrs Moore. 'What a disgrace.' The motorist had pushed the goggles up onto their forehead and carried their driving gloves in one hand.

'The motorist is a lady,' Lottie whispered to Mrs Moore.

'Really?' She peered through her lorgnette at the new arrival. 'I thought she was a man. With some modern women these days, you can't really tell, can you?'

A waiter showed the motorist to the table next to them.

'Bonjour.' She raised her motoring gloves in a wave.

'Oh, bonjour!' said Mrs Moore.

'American?'

'Yes. Is it that obvious?'

'I recognised your accent. I've spent some time in America, you see. I'm Beatrice de Cambry de Baudimont.'

'Golly, what an impressive name!'

'It's Belgian. Just call me Beatrice. I get fed up with explaining to people how to pronounce the rest.' She pulled her goggles and hat off her head and ran a hand through her short, wavy hair. She had blue wide-set eyes, freckles and looked about forty.

'Well, I'm Mrs Roberta Moore and this is my assistant, Miss Lottie Sprigg.'

'Sprigg? I like that name.'

'I'm American, as you've gathered, and Lottie is English. She used to work as a maid for my sister, Lady Buckley-Phipps.'

'Whose name sounds almost as complicated as mine.'

'Almost. She married Lord Buckley-Phipps and they live in Fortescue Manor in Shropshire.'

'I've been to Shropshire.'

'You have?'

'Yes, I competed in a hill trial there once.'

'A hill trial?'

'Where you drive a motor car as fast as possible up a hill. Marvellous fun.'

'I can't help noticing you're the lady who drives that red car out there.' Mrs Moore pointed at it through the window.

'That's me!' She grinned.

'I've noticed you drive it quite fast.'

'She's a Bugatti, and she's built to be driven fast. You don't want to be wasting your time driving slowly in her. What's the point of that?'

'Don't you get into trouble with the traffic police?'

'All the time!' Beatrice laughed. 'They've got used to me now.'

'But isn't it a little bit dangerous?'

'Yes, but that's the thrill, isn't it? There's no point in driving fast if it's not dangerous. What a delightful dog.' Her eyes rested on Rosie. 'A corgi?'

'Yes,' replied Lottie.

'Intelligent dogs. Playful too, usually friendly, although you can never be too sure with some. Does she herd things?'

'I've not noticed her herd anything.'

'Interesting. Corgis were traditionally used by Welsh farmers to herd livestock. Lovely dogs. I would like to have a dog, but it would get in the way.'

'Of what?' asked Mrs Moore.

'Me.'

'I see.'

'My life's too busy. Although I'm here on holiday at the moment. I drove here from Bruges last week.'

'How long did that take?'

'Two days. It's about 750 miles. It's a lovely drive down through France, I recommend it.'

'Do you? I don't drive.'

'You should learn. I can teach you, if you like?'

'I'll think about it. So you're here on holiday, you say?'

'Yes, and enjoying every minute. I drive back and forth along the Côte d'Azur each day and play poker in the evenings.'

'In the casino?'

'Where else? I'll be back there again after dinner. Perhaps I'll see you there?'

'In the casino? I don't think so.'

'You've not been?'

'No.'

Beatrice laughed. 'How funny. What's the point of staying in Monte Carlo if you're not going to gamble away your money in the casino?'

Chapter Five

Lottie went out with Rosie before breakfast the following morning and spotted two police cars parked outside the casino.

'I wonder what they're doing there,' she said to her dog. 'Perhaps someone had a bad night and caused some trouble.'

They walked on past to the terraces overlooking the sea. Lottie took in a deep breath, relishing the warmth and sunshine. She strolled around, enjoying the view and allowing Rosie to catch up with all the fresh smells. Then she found the bench where the jacket had been left the previous day and sat down.

'I wonder if he got his jacket back?' she said to Rosie. And then she thought about the threatening note. Had the conflict been resolved now?

A young man walked down the steps and made his way to the bench next to her. He had dark hair and a weary expression. His appearance suggested he worked at an establishment nearby, he was dressed in a white shirt, black trousers and a white apron. He sat down, loosened his bow tie and gave a sigh. Rosie padded over to him and he patted her head.

'What breed of dog is this?' he asked in French.

'A Pembroke Welsh Corgi,' replied Lottie. 'Her name's Rosie.'

He smiled. 'That's a nice name. You're English?'

'Yes.'

'I can speak some English,' he said. 'We have to speak English with some of our guests.'

'You work in a hotel?'

'No, I work at the casino.'

'Are you a croupier?'

'No,' he laughed. 'It will be a long time before I'm a croupier. I just do all the jobs which no one else wants to. Emptying ashtrays, collecting glasses and keeping everything tidy. Sometimes I'm allowed to serve drinks.'

'Do you enjoy it?'

'I did until last night.'

'Was there some trouble? I saw the police cars parked outside.'

'You've not heard?'

'No.'

'A guest was murdered.'

'Really? How horrible!'

'He was an American. His name was Hector Johnson. I'd seen him a few times before, but I didn't know him.'

'What happened?'

'He played a game of poker in a private room with some other guests. Apparently, he was the winner. After everyone had left the room, he went to collect his winnings for the evening, then returned to the room to fetch his reading glasses. He'd left them in there. At closing time, he was found in there, dead on the floor.'

'And he was definitely murdered?'

The young man nodded. 'He was strangled with a curtain rope.'

'Dreadful!'

'It's certainly dreadful. We've never had anything like this happen at the casino before. I've been up all night because the police have been speaking to everyone. They've got no idea who the murderer is. They've got away.'

'Could the murderer have been one of the people Mr Johnson was playing poker with?'

'I don't know. It could have been. Perhaps they saw him go back into the room and followed him.'

'Do you know who he was playing poker with?'

'I don't know. I didn't see. Michel found the body. He was the dealer in the poker game.' He rubbed his hand over his face. 'I need to go home and get some rest now. I've got to be back here at six o'clock this evening.'

'It sounds like you've had a difficult night.'

'It's not been easy. I've encountered the occasional fight in the casino before, but nothing like this.' He got up to leave, then gave her a smile. 'It was nice meeting you and Rosie. My name is Henri.'

'I'm Lottie, nice to meet you. I hope you get a good rest.'

As she watched him walk away, she recalled again the jacket which had been left beneath the bench. The threatening note in the pocket had been written in English, and Henri had told her the murder victim had been American. Could there be a connection?

'I think I need to tell the police about the note,' she said to Rosie. 'Maybe the staff at the casino also saw it and have already told them. But let's check.'

LOTTIE FOUND a policeman on the steps of the casino and told him about the jacket she'd handed to the doorman the previous day. 'There was a note in the pocket,' she added. 'It was written in English and it was a threatening note. It said, "I warned you but you didn't listen, now you're for it."'

The policeman pulled a puzzled expression.

'Please can you let the investigating detective know about it? I realise it might have nothing to do with the murder, but perhaps it belonged to the victim? And perhaps the note was written by the murderer? It could be relevant.'

The policeman took a notebook and pencil from his pocket and handed them to Lottie. 'Write your name down, please,' he said. 'And the name of your hotel. I shall tell Commissaire Verrando about it and maybe he will speak to you.'

After doing so, Lottie returned to the hotel and found Mrs Moore in the restaurant, having breakfast.

'Lottie! You'll never believe what happened in the casino last night! A man was murdered!'

'Yes, I've just found out.'

'Isn't it awful?' She cracked the shell of her boiled egg with the back of her teaspoon. 'It's another reason why I won't set foot in a place like that. Gambling does strange things to people's minds. Isn't it a travesty? Apparently, the victim was an American who ran a company selling labour-saving appliances in Connecticut.'

'Hector Johnson.'

'Was that his name? Horrendous. Presumably he was here for a holiday and then he met his end. Someone turned nasty about losing their money, I expect.'

'I've just told a policeman about the note I found in that jacket.'

Mrs Moore's eyes widened. 'Golly, I'd forgotten about that! It was a horrible note, wasn't it? Very threatening. I wonder if it was Mr Johnson's jacket which you found?'

'It could have been. And if it was, then the murderer must have written that note.'

'You found the jacket yesterday morning and Mr Johnson was murdered at the casino yesterday evening. That means he must have returned to the casino, even though he'd received a threatening note. Why would he do that?'

'Perhaps he didn't realise he was in danger in the casino? Perhaps the note was given to him when he was elsewhere? I wonder if he knew who'd written it? Perhaps he even discussed it with someone?'

'He may have confided in an acquaintance. If that's the case, then I can only hope the police are investigating it. Well, what an awful thing. But there's not a lot you or I can do about it, Lottie. Don't get any ideas about trying to solve this one. We never met Mr Johnson and we barely know anything about him.'

'I found his jacket.'

'You don't know it was his jacket. It could just be a coincidence that a murder has occurred a day after you found a threatening note. And did the note actually threaten murder?'

'It said that he was "for it". Whatever that means.'

'There you go. A vague threat, really, wasn't it? Leave it to the police, Lottie. I'm sure they'll get to the bottom of it soon enough. Now, do you know what I fancy doing while we're here? Going out on a boat. After breakfast, let's go down to the harbour and see if there's a boat we can charter for a day.'

LOTTIE, Mrs Moore and Rosie were just leaving the hotel when a shiny black motor car pulled up in front of them.

'This looks like someone important, Lottie.'

The uniformed chauffeur jumped out and opened a rear door. A man with dark, curly hair climbed out. He was tall and plump, had a moustache which curled at the ends and wore a navy suit with pink pinstripes.

'Prince Manfred!' exclaimed Mrs Moore. 'I wasn't expecting you!'

He gave a bow, took her hand and kissed it. In the meantime, a slight, blue-suited man climbed out of the other side of the car. Lottie recognised him as Prince Manfred's interpreter, Boris.

'Good morning,' said Prince Manfred.

Lottie deduced this was all he was capable of saying in English because Boris spoke next, 'Prince Manfred was most concerned to learn of the dreadful murder at the Monte Carlo casino yesterday evening and he is visiting you this morning to ask how you are faring, Mrs Moore. He hopes you have not been too upset by the tragic events, given that your hotel is in such close proximity to the casino.'

'Please tell Prince Manfred it is extremely thoughtful of him indeed to travel across the harbour and enquire how I'm faring after last night's awful event. Please assure him that my assistant, Lottie, and I are doing well and have not been too affected by it. We were not acquainted with the victim, nor did we experience anything unpleasant or frightening in nature. Although it's deeply upsetting to learn that something so dreadful has happened, we ourselves are thankfully not adversely affected.'

Boris repeated this to the prince in German while Mrs Moore nodded along with a smile.

'Would you like to join us for morning coffee in the hotel lounge?' she asked once Boris had finished.

'Prince Manfred would be delighted.'

THE HOTEL LOUNGE was furnished with elegant white furniture and had tall windows which overlooked the sea.

'Prince Manfred is extremely upset about the murder,' Boris explained once they'd settled themselves into comfortable chairs. 'It occurred only a short while after he left the casino.'

Mrs Moore's jaw dropped. 'Prince Manfred was in the casino yesterday evening? I didn't realise he likes to gamble.'

'Oh yes, the prince adores gambling. This is why Monaco is one of his favourite places. He likes to visit regularly to see his good friend, the Prince of Monaco, and also to visit one of the most famous casinos in the world.'

'I see.' She pursed her lips.

'Have you visited the casino yet, Mrs Moore?'

'No I haven't.'

'Perhaps you would like to?'

'It's not the sort of thing I do. I'm not a gambler, you see.'

'There is no need for you to play at the tables, you could merely visit and enjoy a drink and the atmosphere.'

'I suppose I could.'

'You could even watch Prince Manfred play some games, he's very good, you know. He's won a lot of money over the years.'

'Has he?'

Lottie felt a little sorry for Mrs Moore, she seemed disappointed by the discovery that Prince Manfred liked to gamble. She was clearly torn between affection for the prince and her dislike of casinos and gambling.

'Did the prince see anything untoward at the casino last night?' she asked.

'No, nothing.'

'Did he know the victim, Mr Johnson?'

'He was at the same baccarat table for a few games last night.'

'Was he? And what sort of man was he?'

Boris asked the prince, then translated his reply. 'He found him extremely polite and courteous. We spoke a few words with him after the game and learned he was a successful businessman in America. Perhaps you knew him?'

'No, I didn't know him at all.'

'But he was from America.'

'There are a lot of people in America these days, I'm afraid I don't know them all. Has the prince got any idea who could have harmed Mr Johnson?'

'No, he has no idea at all. He's extremely shocked by it. As is everyone.'

Prince Manfred looked at his watch, then said something to Boris.

'Prince Manfred says he must depart now.'

'Oh, that is a shame, we've barely spoken at all.'

'Prince Manfred says he is looking forward to seeing you again during your stay.'

'Thank you. Please tell the prince that I'm looking forward to seeing him again too. Lottie and I walked up to the palace yesterday. Actually it was more of a climb than a walk, that rock is very steep isn't it? I wondered whether it would be possible to call on the prince while he's staying at the palace?'

'That wouldn't be possible, I'm afraid.'

'Oh.'

'The Prince of Monaco has strict rules about visitors and as Prince Manfred is a guest of his, then he must abide by those rules.'

'Of course. Naturally. I wouldn't expect anything else. Well, I shall wait to hear again from the prince, shall I?'

'Yes, he will be in contact with you again very soon.'

And with those words, the prince and his interpreter were gone.

Chapter Six

LOTTIE, Mrs Moore and Rosie remained in the lounge. Mrs Moore ordered tea, then gave a sigh. 'I never imagined Prince Manfred would be a gambler, Lottie. I'm quite surprised by it. He doesn't seem the type. I can't deny I'm a little disappointed. My second husband had terrible problems with gambling. He's the one who died of drink. It's one reason I disagree with it, I've seen what it does to people. Maybe some people can gamble happily and it never affects their life in a bad way at all. Perhaps I should try to see it in a different light. It would be quite difficult to though, I've only ever known it to bring misfortune on people. Still, when we love someone, then we must accept all the bad things about them as well as the good.

'Not that I'm in love with the prince yet, but I hope to be one day. It's not easy when I discover he likes to gamble. But I suppose it's one downside of getting to know someone better. When you don't know someone very well, you don't know about their little habits and foibles. In every relationship, there's something about a person which irritates another. That's unavoidable, isn't it? In fact, it's quite nice to have some irritating habits in a relationship because that shows how well you know your partner. So perhaps I shouldn't be surprised that I've learned something unfortunate about the prince. Perhaps if he had the love of a good woman, then he would consider giving up gambling? It's the sort of pursuit which bachelors like to enjoy when they have nothing else to occupy their time in the evening. But when they have a wife, well that's different, isn't it? They have someone they can spend their evenings with. They can have long dinners and entertaining conversations. They can play cards without money! They can read books and poetry together and go for walks arm-in-arm on summer evenings. They can listen to gramophone records together and laugh and generally enjoy each other's company. Wouldn't you say that sounds ideal?'

'You paint a lovely picture of a relationship, Mrs Moore.'

'Thank you. I'm only able to do so because I've had several disastrous ones. With each failed marriage, you learn a little more about yourself and what you would like to find in a partner.'

'Prince Manfred is a bachelor,' said Lottie. 'But he's not a young bachelor. Do you think there's a risk that, once he's married, he'll struggle to abandon his bachelor ways?'

'No, not at all. I can imagine he's quite bored with them! Someone can only pursue their own interests for so long, can't they? And then they look for someone to share their life with. That's what everyone does.'

'The prince differs from most people.'

'Yes he does, not everyone has been brought up in a fairy tale castle on a Bavarian hilltop. But he's a human being just like the rest of us, Lottie, and it's only natural that he wants the same things in life.'

Lottie hoped for Mrs Moore's sake that this was true.

Two men entered the lounge, one was the policeman Lottie had spoken to earlier on the steps of the casino. The other was a short, wide, bespectacled man with a grey moustache who Lottie guessed was a senior detective. The policeman pointed at Lottie and the pair made their way towards her.

'I think they want to speak to me about the jacket I found,' said Lottie.

'Golly, they look very serious indeed.'

'Miss Sprigg?' The short, wide man removed his hat to reveal grey, neatly parted hair. 'I'm Commissaire Verrando.' He spoke in French. 'I understand you found Mr Johnson's jacket yesterday.'

'Yes. Is it definitely his jacket?'

'Yes. He collected it from the casino yesterday afternoon. May I?' He gestured at an empty chair.

'Of course.'

The commissaire placed his hat on the table, sat himself down, and told the policeman to return to the casino.

'So the note in Mr Johnson's pocket was written by the murderer?' asked Lottie.

'Just one moment.' He held up a hand to quieten her and pulled a notebook and pen out of his inside pocket. Lottie noticed his eyes were small and blinking, like those of a mole unaccustomed to bright daylight.

'Now then.' He adjusted his spectacles, opened his notebook and took down Lottie's name, age and address in England. She gave him the address of Mrs Moore's London townhouse.

'Have you seen the note?' she asked him.

'What note?'

'There was a note in the inside pocket of Hector Johnson's jacket. It was a threatening note.'

'I didn't know about this.'

Lottie felt a snap of impatience and did her best to calmly explain. 'When I found the jacket, I searched the pockets to see if there were any clues about who owned it. I found an empty wallet, an empty cigar case, a lighter and some coins. In the inside pocket, I found a note. It was written in English and said, "I warned you but you didn't listen, now you're for it."'

The commissaire shook his head. 'That doesn't match what they told me at the casino. I spoke to the man who you handed the jacket to. He took it into the casino and they searched the pockets just as you did. They found no note.'

'Are you sure? It was crumpled up and pushed into the inside pocket.'

The commissaire shook his head again. 'No note was found. Are you sure you're not mistaken, Miss Sprigg?'

'I didn't imagine the note, if that's what you mean. I can remember what was written on it.'

'Well, I don't know what happened to the note.'

'Someone must have taken it out of the pocket.'

'Who?'

'I don't know, someone at the casino. It was in the pocket when I handed the jacket in.'

'Why would someone remove it?'

'Because it predicted what happened.'

The commissaire gave a slow blink. 'So if you're to be believed, Miss Sprigg, someone threatened Mr Johnson, then hid the evidence that they did so. And you think that someone in the casino hid that evidence? So someone in the casino didn't want to incriminate someone. Either themselves or someone else.' He rubbed his nose. 'The trouble is, I need actual evidence and I have no evidence at the moment that the note existed. All I have is your word for it. This makes things difficult.'

'Someone in the casino must have seen that note. They must have removed it from the pocket!'

'According to you, Miss Sprigg. But when I speak to them

in the casino, no one mentions a note. Is this all you wanted to speak to me about?'

'Yes.'

'Did you ever meet Hector Johnson?'

'No.'

'Well, that is a shame.' He folded his notebook closed and put it back into his pocket with his pen. 'I'm sorry to trouble you, Miss Sprigg.'

'But wait, the murderer could have written that note!'

'I'll be the judge of that when I see it.' He stood and put his hat back on. 'Enjoy the rest of your day, ladies.'

Chapter Seven

'WELL THAT CONVERSATION didn't appear to go particularly well,' said Mrs Moore once the commissaire had departed. She didn't understand French, so Lottie explained to her what had just been discussed.

'The note has gone missing?' she said. 'Perhaps Mr Johnson destroyed it, it's not the sort of note you want to keep, is it?'

'The detective told me the casino staff didn't find the note in the pocket.'

'Who did you give the jacket to?'

'A doorman.'

'So he must have taken the note out of the pocket?'

'He could have.'

'Why would he?'

'To protect the murderer, I suppose. Or perhaps it wasn't him, perhaps it was the next person he handed the jacket to. They could have found the note and destroyed it.'

'Then omitted to tell the police about it? It sounds like someone at the casino is covering something up. You've done all you can, Lottie. You've told the detective about the note and he can follow it up with the casino.'

BEATRICE DE CAMBRY DE BAUDIMONT joined them for lunch. She wore a checked shirt and slacks. 'Shame about the man who was strangled in the casino last night,' she said.

'Were you there?' asked Mrs Moore.

'Oh yes.'

'Goodness. Did you see or hear anything?'

'No nothing. It happened after I left. The first thing I knew about it was this morning.'

'Did you know the man at all?'

'Yes, I played poker with him. In the same room he was later murdered in.'

'Golly, really? How awful for you!'

'Not really, I wasn't there when it happened.'

'But the thought is still awful, though.'

'Yes, I suppose it is.'

'What was he like?'

'He was an American businessman who sold household appliances. I don't know how old he was, about thirty-five maybe. Fair hair... I suppose you could describe him as quite handsome. A bit of a salesman though, he couldn't resist telling me all about one of his vacuum cleaners. As if I'd have any interest in one of those! I suppose I'd describe him as pleasant but dull. And a bit annoying too. And he won the poker game.'

'Who do you think murdered him?'

'I've no idea.'

'Could it have been one of the people he played poker with? Perhaps they were annoyed he won their money?'

'It's possible, but that would be a strange thing to do.

Everyone goes into a poker game knowing they might lose, so why take it out on the winner in that way?'

A waiter took their order. 'Steak tartare for me,' said Beatrice in French. 'And a bottle of your finest Châteauneuf-du-Pape.'

'I understood the last bit of what you said there,' said Mrs Moore. 'Isn't that a wine?'

'Yes. What's good enough for the pope is good enough for me.'

'The pope?'

'Châteauneuf-du-Pape is the name of a village which the pope chose for his summer residency about 700 years ago. He had the area planted up with vineyards and produced the wine I love so much today. This was in the days when the papacy was in Avignon.'

'Where's that?'

'Close to Châteauneuf-du-Pape, of course. The other side of Nice from here, about 180 miles away. I could probably cover it in half a day.'

'I'm sure you could. So we have a pope to thank for some nice wine?'

'That's right. Popes have their uses.'

'How many of you were playing poker?' Lottie asked.

'There were five of us.'

'You, Mr Johnson and who else?'

'There was a French couple and a young woman. We were introduced, but I can't remember their names. I think the French couple were from Paris. The young woman wasn't French, she was... oh, English, I think. Rich father. We were in a private room which is provided for trusted guests who have a little more money than usual to spend. More money and higher stakes.'

Beatrice didn't look wealthy, but Lottie reasoned she

earned good money from her motor races. Her sporty Bugatti car was no doubt expensive.

'I heard everyone left the room once the game had finished, but Mr Johnson returned to fetch his reading glasses,' said Lottie.

'That's right.'

'And the murderer was lying in wait for him there?'

'Apparently so. There are some big velvet curtains in that room and I heard the murderer hid behind them. It explains how they got hold of the curtain rope too. What a brutal thing to do to someone.'

Although Beatrice clearly hadn't known Mr Johnson well, Lottie had expected her to be a little more shocked or upset about the murder. Instead, she seemed rather blasé about it.

Chapter Eight

LATER THAT AFTERNOON, Beatrice de Cambry de Baudimont sat in Commissaire Verrando's office. She was supposed to be going out for an afternoon drive, but instead she was stuck in a stuffy room, having to explain herself to a dozy detective. It was ruining her holiday. And all because a vacuum cleaner salesman had got himself murdered in the casino.

'How long are you in Monaco for?' asked the bespectacled commissaire. Beatrice noticed his chair was much higher than hers so he could look down on her. The effect would have felt intimidating if he hadn't been so languorous and sleepy-eyed.

'I arrived here last week,' she said. 'And I'll stay here until I've lost all my money. So I could be here another week or another day. No one can predict what will happen at the tables, can they?'

'Indeed not.'

'Do you like to gamble, Commissaire?'

'Only visitors to Monaco may gamble. Those of us who live here are forbidden to do so.'

'I'd forgotten about that rule! It doesn't seem fair.'

'It is tradition.' A long pause followed while he looked through some papers on his desk. She gritted her teeth with impatience as she waited for him to speak again. Eventually he did. 'You are aware that you must remain in Monaco while this investigation is underway?'

'But Monaco's so small! Can't I at least drive about the French Riviera?'

He sighed. 'Where are you staying?'

'At the Hôtel de Paris.'

'Then you must spend every night there, or at another hotel in Monaco, while this investigation is underway. You can drive about in the day, but you stay here at night. Is that clear?'

'Yes.' She couldn't imagine the investigation proceeding quickly under his command.

'When did you first meet Mr Hector Johnson?'

An image flashed into her mind of their unfortunate meeting in Rhode Island. She pushed it away and answered with as much confidence as possible. 'When we played poker yesterday evening.'

He blinked slowly, then wrote this down. He hadn't seemed to notice her lie. Perhaps this interview wouldn't be too difficult after all.

'And did you speak to him yesterday evening?' he asked.

'Yes, because I was playing poker with him. But not much because I don't like talking when I'm playing. Mr Johnson was being too talkative in my opinion, and it was a distraction at times. Perhaps he did it intentionally.'

'What was he talking about?'

'Vacuum cleaners. And a new electric washing machine. He had lots to say about his labour-saving devices, but I'm not interested in any of them. I'm not the sort of lady to keep house. I'm either in a hotel or a motor car and that's the way I like it. I've got no interest in buying something from a businessman in Connecticut.'

'How did you know he was from Connecticut?'

'Because he told me.'

'Did he talk about anything else?'

'Not really. He may have done, but I wasn't really listening to him half the time. I was only interested in the game.'

'Did you suspect Mr Johnson was in danger?'

'No, why would I suspect that?'

'He didn't mention anything about his life being in danger?'

'No. And that would be an odd thing to mention during a poker game, wouldn't it? He didn't know any of us, so I think it would've been strange if he'd suddenly told us such a thing.'

'Were you aware of him upsetting anyone?'

'He upset me a little because he kept talking and it was distracting. I think he annoyed the other players a bit too. But no one was upset enough to murder him. That would have been an inappropriate response.'

The commissaire looked at his notes again. 'Just to be clear, you were playing poker with Hector Johnson, Joseph Rochefort, Marie Rochefort and Grace Harrison?'

'I can't exactly remember the other names, but that sounds about right.'

'And how were the other players with him?'

'It was difficult to discern their exact feelings because everyone was wearing their best poker face. I suspect he annoyed them as much as he annoyed me with his talking. The other three didn't enter into much conversation with him. In the end, he was directing most of his conversation at the dealer who was responding only out of politeness.'

'Was there anything which occurred during that poker game which seemed to you unusual?'

'No, nothing at all.'

'And what time did you leave the casino?'

'After the game finished, just after two o'clock this morning.'

'Did you leave with anyone else?'

'No, I was on my own.'

'And where did you go after you left the casino?'

'I went back to my hotel and went to bed.'

'Is there anyone who can vouch for that?'

'I don't know. Possibly a doorman at the casino or a doorman or receptionist at the hotel. I wasn't with anyone else.'

The commissaire sat back in his chair and surveyed her with his bespectacled little eyes. 'So you never met Hector Johnson before the poker game yesterday evening?'

'Never. I had no idea who he was.'

She wasn't going to mention the incident from the previous week. And as she thought about it now, she was revisited by the rage she'd felt when she'd unexpectedly seen his face.

Such anger!

As far as Beatrice was concerned, Hector Johnson had got what he'd deserved.

Chapter Nine

LOTTIE TOOK Rosie out for a stroll before dinner, hoping she might bump into Henri as he returned to work at the casino that evening. She wanted to find out if he knew anything more about the murder.

Mrs Moore had told her to leave the investigation to the police, but Lottie couldn't help feeling inquisitive. Although she'd never met Hector Johnson, the threatening note in his jacket intrigued her. And Beatrice's nonchalance about the murder confused her. Was it characteristic of Beatrice? Or did she have something to hide?

Lottie and Rosie wandered about the terraces, enjoying the warm evening air. Rosie played with a chihuahua called Claude for a bit, then Lottie caught sight of Henri walking up the road from the harbour.

'Oh, hello.' His grin was more handsome than she'd remembered. 'Lottie, isn't it? And Rosie.' He patted the corgi on the head.

'That's right. In fact, I was hoping I'd bump into you.'

'You were?'

'Only because I forgot to tell you about a jacket I found

yesterday morning which belonged to Mr Johnson. Have you got a few minutes to talk before you start work?'

He nodded, and Lottie told him about the jacket and the threatening note. 'The trouble is,' she added. 'The staff in the casino say there was no note in the jacket pocket.'

'What did the doorman look like?' he asked.

'He had a large chin.'

Henri laughed.

'What's so funny?'

'I've not heard Louis described like that before.'

'So you know who I mean from that quick description?'

'Yes, I know who you mean. Louis is nice, I can't imagine him hiding the note and I can't think why he'd want to. I can ask him about it and find out who he gave the jacket to. It sounds strange, though. The note was threatening to kill Hector Johnson?'

'The person who wrote the note said he would be "for it". That means some trouble, doesn't it? Possibly murder.'

'I wonder why the note was written. And I wonder why it went missing too.'

'Have you come across Beatrice de Cambry de Baudimont?'

'No, who's she?'

'She drives a noisy red motor car. She's Belgian and, from what she's told me and my employer, I think she's a racing driver.'

'I know exactly who you mean now. She nearly hit Monsieur Blanchard, the casino manager, when she was parking in Place du Casino last week.'

'Oh dear, she seems to drive quite dangerously. She told us she played poker with Mr Johnson last night.'

Henri's eyes widened. 'She was in the private room?'

'Yes, but she said she left before he was attacked.'

'She would say that, wouldn't she? The murderer isn't exactly going to admit to having been in the room at the time.'

'That's a good point. I'm wondering if she's the murderer.'

'I've seen the way she drives about and I've seen her in the casino. But I don't know her and I've never spoken to her. I couldn't say whether she's the murderer or not.'

'She said that she and Mr Johnson played poker with a French couple and a young woman.'

'I don't know who they could be. I'll be able to find out more this evening, though. I'll speak to some of my colleagues and find out what they've seen and heard. You seem quite interested in what happened to Mr Johnson.'

'That's because I found his jacket with that note in the pocket. And the note appears to have been hidden by someone. Possibly even destroyed. I think that person is protecting the murderer.'

'An interesting thought. Do you often puzzle over things like this?'

'I do. I like reading detective stories and I've managed to work out a few puzzles in real life too.'

'Such as what?'

Lottie gave him a brief description of her time in Venice, Paris and Cairo. Henri's mouth was hanging open by the time she'd finished.

'I don't know what to say,' he said. 'That's astonishing. Do you really think you could solve Mr Johnson's murder, too?'

'I don't know. I never knew him, so it's difficult.'

'I'll try to help where I can.'

'Will you? That's very kind.'

'It interests me too.' He stepped nearer and lowered his voice. 'Between you and me, I've not got a lot of confidence in Commissaire Verrando. Apparently, all he wants to do is retire. I think it would be better if he did so and let someone better do the job. Unfortunately, I don't think they're willing to employ a young English girl.'

'I'm not that young!'

'How old are you? Nineteen?'

'Yes? How did you know?'

'Just a good guess.' He grinned, then added, 'I'm only a year older than you. I'll see what I can find out and let you know.'

LOTTIE AND MRS MOORE dined again in the hotel restaurant that evening.

'I had hoped for an invitation to the palace, but nothing's turned up yet,' said Mrs Moore as she sliced a bread roll in half. 'I can only hope that Prince Manfred will ask the Prince of Monaco if I can be a guest. Wouldn't that be something? Mind you, I wouldn't know what to wear. I don't think I've got anything suitable.'

Lottie thought of all the luggage they'd been hauling around with them and wondered how that could be possible.

'I might have to pop into one of the little boutique shops they have here and choose something. Wouldn't that be fun? But there's no point if I don't receive an invitation.' She sighed and surveyed their fellow diners through her lorgnette. 'I can see our lady motorist friend over there,' she commented. 'Do you see her, Lottie? In the blue blouse. She's rather eccentric, isn't she? She's clearly knowledgeable about a number of topics such as dog breeds, wine and motor cars, but her manner's rather direct, isn't it? I can imagine her upsetting people with her bluntness. Now here's a thought.' Mrs Moore lowered her voice. 'Do you think she could have murdered the American salesman? She seemed quite unbothered about him when we spoke to her earlier, didn't she? And she was keen to say it had happened after she'd left. But what if she didn't leave before he was murdered? Perhaps she was the one hiding behind the curtain? Oh golly, she's seen me staring at her now.' Mrs Moore lowered her lorgnette, forced a smile and returned Beatrice's wave. 'And now she's coming over here.'

'I spotted you spying on me, Mrs Moore!' said Beatrice with a grin, her hands shoved into the pockets of her trousers.

'Oh, I wasn't spying, I was—'

'I know, I was only joking.' She turned to Lottie. 'You asked me who was playing the poker game, didn't you? And I couldn't remember their names. The commissaire interviewed me this afternoon, and he reminded me. Rochefort.'

'Rochefort?'

'Yes, that's the name of the French couple. He also told me the name of the young English woman, but I've forgotten that again. If I remember, I'll tell you. Madame and Monsieur Rochefort are from Paris. A fashionable couple, as you might expect, and she's quite a beauty. They were both well-dressed but rather pale. The sea air down here should put some colour in their cheeks. Like me, they'll be stuck in Monaco until the commissaire completes his investigation. I think we could all grow old and grey before that happens!'

Chapter Ten

THE FOLLOWING MORNING, Joseph Rochefort sat up tall in his seat. But it wasn't tall enough to compensate for the height of Commissaire Verrando's chair. It annoyed him that the detective could look down on him and make him feel inferior. Joseph's wife, Marie, didn't seem bothered. She reclined in her chair, one leg crossed over the other, and inhaled on her cigarette holder.

'So to summarise our discussions so far,' said the commissaire. 'You didn't see anyone acting suspiciously during the poker game with Hector Johnson.'

'That's right.' Joseph checked his watch. Half an hour of the interview had already passed, and it was a complete waste of his time.

'And we have also established that both you and Madame Rochefort knew Hector Johnson.'

'Yes, but not very well. As I've already explained, he approached me after he visited our department store in Paris. He wanted to supply us with household appliances.'

'And you arranged to meet him in Monaco to discuss the plan?'

'That's right.' Joseph turned to his wife and rolled his eyes. They'd already been through this with the sleepy detective.

'Why Monaco?' asked the commissaire.

'Because it's a nice place.'

'But why not Paris? That's a nice place too.'

'Because...' Joseph's mind stumbled as he tried to come up with a legitimate reason. 'My wife and I wanted a break from the department store and we decided we'd like some time by the sea. And where better than Monaco? It has the luxury hotels and high-class leisure pursuits which we enjoy. And we fancied the drive, too. We drove here from Paris.'

'How long did that take?'

'Two days. We stayed overnight in Lyon.'

The commissaire nudged his spectacles up his nose and examined some papers on his desk. Joseph turned to his wife, and she pulled an exasperated expression. If she was upset by Hector's death, she didn't show it. In fact, it was difficult to know what his wife thought about anything these days. She'd become unreadable in recent months. Was it possible she was having another affair?

'Have you heard of Philippe Albertini?' asked the commissaire.

'What?' Joseph startled at the name. 'Who's he?'

'You've not heard of him?'

'I don't think so... no.' Joseph felt his heart thud heavily in his chest. What did this lethargic detective know about Albertini?

'Perhaps you didn't realise who he was when you spoke to him?' said the commissaire.

'I spoke to him? When?'

'In the casino last night.'

'Oh.' Who had seen him? Was he being watched? If so, then he would look foolish if he flatly denied everything. 'I've just remembered who Albertini is now,' he said. 'I apologise. It must be your accent, I didn't recognise the name when you first said it. I did speak with a gentleman called Philippe Albertini in the casino. We were at the same roulette table for a while.'

'Do you know who he is?'

'No, I don't know who he is at all.'

'My men came across two undercover French policemen yesterday. They're from Marseille.'

Marie gave a splutter.

'Are you alright, darling?' Joseph asked her.

'I'm fine. It's the air in here, it's a bit... close.' She wafted a long-fingered hand in front of her face.

'It certainly is. Hopefully, we won't be detained for much longer.' He turned back to the commissaire. 'Two undercover policemen from Marseille, you say?'

'Yes. When confronted, they admitted they were watching a known criminal from Marseille, Philippe Albertini.'

'But that's shocking!'

'It certainly is. They should have had the permission of the commissioner before working undercover here.'

'No, I mean about Albertini being a criminal. I had no idea!'

'I feel it is my duty to warn you about him. He's suspected of being involved in fraud, racketeering and importing heroin from Turkey.'

'Really?' Joseph feigned surprise. 'I knew nothing about that!'

'You would be well advised to stay away from the man.'

'He seems such a well-mannered gentleman.'

'Many crooks are, Monsieur Rochefort.'

'You say he's suspected of crimes, has anything been proven?'

'You'll have to ask the police in Marseille about that. However, my men are now watching the French policemen who are watching Albertini and it was observed that you had quite a long conversation with Albertini last night. May I ask what it was about?'

'Erm...' Joseph searched his mind for ideas. 'Art.'

'Art?'

'We both appreciate art. We talked about the pieces we've collected over the years. But now that you've told me he's a criminal, I can only imagine he stole his!' He laughed in an attempt to lighten the mood.

'As I've said, take my advice and stay away from him,' said Commissaire Verrando. 'You don't want to be in more trouble than you already are.'

'I'm sorry, I'm in trouble, am I?'

'Well, perhaps not you. But certainly your wife.'

'Marie? What's she done wrong?'

The commissaire didn't reply. Instead, he bent down behind his desk and Joseph heard a drawer opening. Then the commissaire reappeared and held up a silver cigarette case in his hand.

'Do you recognise this, Madame Rochefort?'

'No.'

Clever woman, what a good reply, thought Joseph.

'You don't recognise it?' said the commissaire. 'But I believe it's yours.'

'What makes you say that?'

'It has a message engraved on the back.' The commissaire squinted through his glasses as he read it, '"To my darling Marie, from your loving husband, Joseph Rochefort."'

Perhaps not so clever after all, thought Joseph.

'Oh,' said Marie. 'It was the way you were holding it. It made it look different.'

'Do you know where this was found, Madame Rochefort?'

'No.'

'Next to Hector Johnson's body.'

'What? I haven't the faintest idea how it got there.'

'It's a very nice cigarette case. I'm surprised you didn't report it missing.'

Chapter Eleven

A WAITER HANDED Mrs Moore an envelope at breakfast the following morning.

'Is this what I think it is?' she said, gleefully ripping it open. Lottie watched her eyes scan the piece of paper inside, and then a smile broke out across her face. 'Yes, it is! It's from Prince Manfred! He's invited me to the er... I actually have no idea how to say it. What is it, Lottie?' She handed the piece of paper to her.

'L'Institut océanographique de Monaco.'

'What is it? Something to do with the ocean?'

'Yes, the Oceanographic Institute.'

'Oh. Well, that doesn't seem very exciting. I can only guess the prince likes oceans and I suppose I shall have to show some interest in them too. It says here the car will pick me up at eleven.' She checked her watch. 'That's in an hour's time. It's not a great deal of notice, is it? Oh well, I shan't grumble. Instead, I'm happy the prince has got in touch! There's only one problem, Lottie, I think this invitation is only intended for me. Now that the prince and I know each other a little better, I think...' She trailed off and bit her lip.

'That's absolutely fine, Mrs Moore. Rosie and I can entertain ourselves.'

'Can you?'

'Yes, of course!'

'Alright then. And before the day is out, I shall be able to tell you all about oceans.'

After Lottie had helped Mrs Moore choose a suitable outfit for the day and waved her off in a shiny black car, she had a moment to think.

Beatrice had given her the name Rochefort. Where were Madame and Monsieur Rochefort now? Beatrice had suggested they had to remain in Monaco until the investigation was complete. Lottie stood on the hotel steps with Rosie and pondered this. 'I wonder what Madame and Monsieur Rochefort think about Mr Johnson's death?' she said to her dog. 'Perhaps they saw something suspicious? Perhaps they were even responsible for it?'

The only way to find out more was to meet them. And to do that, Lottie had to find them. She reasoned that if the Rocheforts had been playing poker in the private room, then they were wealthy. And if they were wealthy, then it was likely they were staying in one of Monaco's best hotels.

'Perhaps they're staying in this hotel?' Lottie said to Rosie. 'Let's ask at reception.' The pair left the steps and went into the lobby, where three receptionists sat behind a long polished desk.

She approached the friendliest looking one, a lady with neat, bobbed hair. 'Are Monsieur and Madame Rochefort staying here?' she asked in French.

'I don't think so. Let me check.' She leafed through a large book. 'No, we don't have them staying with us.'

'I wonder where they're staying? Knowing them, they'll be

staying in a hotel as nice as this one. But not quite as good, obviously.' She smiled.

'You could try the Hôtel Metropole or the Hôtel Hermitage. They're both very nice hotels, just not as nice as this one, like you say.' The receptionist returned her smile.

'Thank you, I'll do that. Would you mind telling me where they are?'

The receptionist gave Lottie directions and, as luck would have it, both hotels were close by.

'I LIKE the fact Monaco is very small,' Lottie said to Rosie as they walked around the back of the Hôtel de Paris to the Hôtel Hermitage. 'It means that everywhere is accessible on foot.' The hotel was an ornate five storey building of cream stone with elegant wrought-iron balconies. Inside, the marbled lobby echoed with polite chatter and was furnished with stylish seating and potted palms.

Lottie planned to ask the Rocheforts about Hector Johnson's jacket. She wasn't expecting them to tell her much about it, but the topic was the only connection she had to the case. Once she'd asked them about it, she hoped they might go on to tell her some new information.

She also recalled the headed paper the threatening note had been written on had come from the Hôtel Hermitage. If the Rocheforts were staying in this hotel, could one of them have written the note?

She approached the reception desk. 'I wish to speak with Madame and Monsieur Rochefort, please.'

'Of course,' replied a young man with a moustache. He consulted the book in front of him. 'Do you know which room they're staying in?'

'I'm afraid I don't.'

He continued to look through the book. 'Actually, we don't appear to have any guests of that name staying here.'

'Oh?' Lottie feigned surprise. 'This is the Hôtel Metropole, isn't it?' She deliberately made the error in the hope she wouldn't seem too suspicious.

'No.' He gave a thin smile. 'This is the Hôtel Hermitage.'

'I'm so sorry. I confused the two hotels.'

'Not a problem at all. You'll find the Hôtel Metropole by the Cafe de Paris.'

Lottie thanked him and went on her way with Rosie.

'I hope they're staying at the Metropole,' she said to her dog. 'If not, then we'll have to try some other hotels.'

They crossed the Place du Casino and Rosie took an interest in some people sitting at the tables outside the Cafe de Paris. She received a few pats on the head and a piece of someone's biscuit.

Lottie wondered if she could rule out Madame and Monsieur Rochefort from having written the threatening note. If they weren't staying at the Hôtel Hermitage, then surely neither of them had access to its headed paper? That left one more poker player who could have been staying there, a young English woman, and Beatrice couldn't remember her name. Lottie hoped she'd recall it soon.

At the Hôtel Metropole, she made her way to the reception desk and asked if she could speak to Madame and Monsieur Rochefort.

'Of course,' said the sleek-haired receptionist. 'I shall telephone their room, actually...' She looked past Lottie's shoulder. 'Here they are now.'

'Really?' Lottie gulped, preparing herself for the conversation.

'Madame and Monsieur Rochefort!' The receptionist called them over. 'This young lady would like to speak with you.'

Lottie forced a smile onto her face and turned to look at the couple. Madame Rochefort was tall with wavy, fair hair and dark eyes. She wore a coral pink dress, a matching jacket and a lot of jewellery. She was remarkably beautiful, but her expression was imperious, which Lottie found intimidating and a little unlikeable. Monsieur Rochefort had a long thin face and pointed features, he didn't look the sort of man who smiled very often. His hair was dark, and he wore a smart suit.

The pair strode towards her now and the heels of Madame Rochefort's shoes echoed on the marble tiled floor.

Lottie did her best to appear confident as the Rocheforts took up position in front of her. The French lady noticed Rosie and a faint smile played on her lips. 'Sweet dog.'

'Her name's Rosie.'

'That's a nice name.'

'And I'm Lottie Sprigg, it's nice to meet you.'

'You're English? You speak good French.'

'Thank you.'

'What do you want to speak to us about?' asked Monsieur Rochefort.

'I understand you played poker with Hector Johnson the other evening.'

They both frowned. 'How do you know that?' asked Monsieur Rochefort.

'I have a friend who works at the casino who told me. I'm wondering whether you know if Mr Johnson was reunited with his jacket?'

'Why would we know that?'

'Was he wearing it when you were playing?'

'He was wearing a jacket,' said Madame Rochefort. 'But I don't know whether or not it was the one you're referring to.'

'I found his jacket under a bench and handed it in to the casino and I want to find out if he received it.'

'Can't your friend at the casino tell you?'

'Strangely, he can't.'

'I'm sorry, Miss Sprigg, but I'm not sure we can help you,' said Monsieur Rochefort. 'I hope you don't mind me saying it, but this is a strange question to ask.'

'Yes, it is. I'm sorry, Monsieur and Madame Rochefort. I only wanted to make sure that his jacket was returned to him before he died. It was very distressing to hear about his murder.' Lottie made her lower lip wobble, and she noticed a flicker of concern in Madame Rochefort's eyes.

'It was very distressing indeed,' said the French lady. 'The attack took place after we'd left the casino. Did you know him well?'

'No, I didn't know him at all. I just found his jacket.'

'I see.'

'Well, I'm sorry we can't be of more help,' said Monsieur Rochefort, taking his wife's arm.

'Do you know who could have harmed him?' Lottie said, keen to ask the question before they left.

Monsieur Rochefort scowled. 'No. Why would we know that?'

'I'm just wondering if you saw anything suspicious or perhaps Hector Johnson hinted at something?'

'No, nothing at all. Now excuse us, we have a busy day. We've already had our time wasted by the police this morning and we have lots to be getting on with.'

'Of course, thank you for your time.'

Chapter Twelve

MARIE ROCHEFORT WATCHED the English girl and her dog leave the hotel lobby.

'What was all that about?' asked her husband. 'Why was she asking us about Hector Johnson's jacket?'

'I don't know.' She released herself from his grip on her arm and they began to walk back to their room. 'She must know something.'

'Such as what?'

'I've no idea. But she told us she knows someone at the casino, didn't she?'

'Who? Blanchard?'

'We could have asked her who it was, couldn't we? But you ended the conversation.'

'That's because I felt wary of her.'

'A young English girl?'

'Yes! We've already found out there are undercover French police watching Albertini. What if she's here watching some-one, too?'

'She's not watching Albertini.'

'How can you be so sure?'

She couldn't let on to her husband how she knew this. 'They wouldn't employ a girl to do that. And she's English.'

'But maybe they would? And perhaps she's pretending to be English? She could be a spy, Marie.'

There was little doubt that Joseph had been shaken up by the discovery he'd been watched in the casino while he'd met with Albertini.

They turned into a thickly carpeted corridor and Marie sighed. Her plan was going wrong. The French police were supposed to be gathering evidence that her husband and Philippe Albertini were conspiring to run a racketeering business together. Now Joseph knew they were being watched and there was a risk he'd tell Albertini too. If that happened, then Albertini would probably go into hiding somewhere and the entire plan would fall flat. And to think she'd worked so hard for this! She just wanted to be free from her husband and his criminal scheming.

'And she asked if we knew who could have harmed Hector!' said Joseph. 'What a question. Why does she think we'd know the answer to that?'

'Because we were in the room with him.'

'It's regretful there weren't more of us playing poker that evening. Not only would we have had a better poker game, but people wouldn't be pointing the finger at us as they are.'

'People can point their fingers all they like, but they can't do anything more without evidence.'

'It doesn't help that your cigarette case was found next to his body.'

'I don't know how that happened!'

'And you denied it was yours and it happened to be the case I'd given you for our wedding anniversary!'

'You were the one who had it engraved with a message.'

'I had no idea you were going to drop it at the scene of a murder!'

'I didn't drop it there!'

'So how did it get there?'

'I don't know!'

'Somehow we're going to have to explain all this to Albertini. But it's going to be very difficult if he's got policemen following him about. What a mess! It was a mistake to try to do business with Hector Johnson. He was clearly the wrong man all along.' He stopped in the corridor. 'Do you know why I chose him?'

'Why?'

'Because of you.'

'Me?'

'Yes. And the fondness you had for him.'

'What fondness?'

'I wasn't born yesterday, Marie. I know how you felt about him when we met him in Paris.'

Had it been that obvious? Marie felt her face heat up. 'I liked him,' she said. 'But not in that way.'

'Even so, you were the bait to draw him in. But now it's all gone wrong. What are we going to do?'

'Nothing. Before long, he'll be forgotten about.'

'Not in Connecticut, he won't be.'

'That's all the way over in America.'

'Which is not so far away these days.'

She put her hand in his. She had to calm him down and hopefully get her plan back on course. 'You worry too much, darling,' she said softly.

'Do I?'

'Yes. You know you do. Everything will work out, we just need to leave things to settle down a bit. The commissaire isn't exactly going to do much, is he? You can tell he's not completely with it. I'm sure something else will distract him and his men before long and he'll give up bothering with Hector Johnson.'

'And what about Blanchard? It doesn't look good for his casino. He'll be looking for someone to blame.'

'Then perhaps we give him someone to blame?'

'Who?'

'I don't know yet, darling, I'll think about it.'

He gave her a smile. 'I know what you're like when you put your mind to things, Marie.'

'Exactly.' She leaned in and kissed him on the cheek. 'We'll find a solution. We always do.'

Chapter Thirteen

'I CAN'T PRETEND the Oceanographic Institute was interesting,' said Mrs Moore when she returned to the hotel that afternoon. 'But it was fun spending the day with Prince Manfred. And the building is built into the side of the cliff so there are some wonderful views of the sea.'

'What did you see there?'

'Models of boats and sea creatures, some skeletons of dolphins or whales or something or other and an awful lot of descriptions of things which Prince Manfred asked Boris to translate for him. He insisted on wanting to hear about everything! Fortunately, there were a few places where I could sit and have a rest. But there's more excitement this evening because guess where the prince has invited me?'

'Where?'

'The casino of all places. I can't say I'm particularly fussed about going there, but I suppose it will be interesting to see what it's like. I'm not parting with any of my money though. Would you like to accompany us? I can't imagine I'll be spending a great deal of time with the prince because he'll be absorbed in all those games they have there.'

Lottie hadn't imagined she would see inside the casino and she was interested in finding out what it was like. 'Yes, I'd like to come!'

'Wonderful! The prince will meet us outside the hotel at eight o'clock. But we have to wear something smart and I don't think you have anything suitable in your wardrobe.'

'I have the turquoise dress we bought in Paris.'

'No, it needs to be something fancier than that. I've spotted a rather nice dress shop on the road down to the harbour, let's have a look in there now and get you something for this evening. And after that, I shall need a nap. It's already been a tiring day and I expect it's going to be a late night tonight. I don't know where Prince Manfred gets his energy from. How's your day been?'

'Quite peaceful. Rosie and I went for a walk and then I read my book for a while.'

'That sounds very nice indeed.'

Lottie didn't want to tell Mrs Moore she'd met the Rocheforts because she'd scold her for snooping. Although Lottie felt proud of how she'd managed to find them, the conversation with them had been uncomfortable. She wished now she'd planned it more and found a better excuse for speaking with them. If they'd had nothing to do with Hector Johnson's death, Lottie imagined they'd probably forget about her impromptu visit. But if they did have something to do with it, there was a risk her visit had antagonised them. Had she been foolish? She worried now that she had.

'ARE YOU ALRIGHT, LOTTIE?' asked Mrs Moore as they walked with Rosie to the dress shop. 'You seem quiet.'

'I'm fine.'

'Oh good. It wouldn't surprise me if you're feeling weary

from all our travelling. It can take it out of you, can't it? I can only hope Prince Manfred stays put for some time in Monaco, so we have some time to recover ourselves.'

They passed the broken wall which was now being repaired by two men. Rosie sniffed at the tools they'd propped up against the wall then wagged her tail as she requested to say hello to the men.

'They're busy,' Lottie said to her. But one of the men had spotted Rosie, and he approached her and patted her on the head.

'What a friendly dog,' he said in French. 'A corgi?'

'Yes,' she replied. 'What happened to the wall?'

'A motor car knocked into it.'

'Oh dear, that was careless of someone.'

'It could have been worse, apparently they nearly hit a pedestrian.'

'It's lucky they didn't.'

'Some people don't know how to drive. They treat the road like a racetrack.'

Lottie smiled, mindful of a motorist she knew who did such a thing.

IN THE DRESS SHOP, two glamorous assistants were happy to help Lottie choose a new dress. They spoke good English and were soon deep in discussion with Mrs Moore about what Lottie would look best in.

'She has a lovely complexion,' said one. Her eyes were edged with dark eyeliner.

'Her hair is a little flat,' said the other. 'She should wear something on her head to divert attention from it.'

'I'm envious of her slim figure,' said Mrs Moore.

'Very fashionable at the moment,' said the assistant with

dark eyeliner. 'And she must make the most of it because a slim figure doesn't last forever.'

'We all get fat one day,' said the other.

'And some of us have always been that way,' said Mrs Moore. 'It's why I won't give up my old-fashioned corsets.'

They all laughed, and Lottie was given a long laurel green dress to try on. It was made of silk and had a section of fabric which draped across the front and tied at the left hip in an enormous bow.

'No,' said the assistant with dark eyeliner. 'It looks all wrong.'

'Really?' said Lottie. 'I like it.'

A marmalade orange dress was thrust at her. This one had a low waist and a full skirt with elaborate beaded embroidery on its hem.

'Now I like this one!' said Mrs Moore when Lottie stepped out of the changing cubicle. 'Give us a twirl!'

Lottie liked the way the skirt swished around her legs but the assistant with dark eyeliner was still unimpressed. 'You need to sparkle.' With these words, she strode across the shop and found a floor-length crimson gown decorated with sequins.

'Oh yes!' Mrs Moore clapped her hands together. 'That's very Monte Carlo!'

Lottie couldn't imagine wearing something so glamorous. 'But it's entirely above my station,' she protested.

'Station?' said Mrs Moore. 'Let's forget about your days as a maid in Shropshire. You're in Monaco now, Lottie! It's a very English trait to be so preoccupied with class and what one is and isn't entitled to do. Forget about that and wear a beautiful dress. You'll turn heads in it!'

'I don't think I want to turn heads.'

'Oh come now, everyone wants to turn heads.'

Lottie went into the changing cubicle and pulled the dress

on. It fitted perfectly. She barely recognised the glamorous young woman in the mirror. It didn't seem possible for an orphan from a little town in England to look like this. Tears prickled her eyes. Embarrassed by the strength of her emotions, she swiftly wiped them away.

Chapter Fourteen

PRINCE MANFRED'S LARGE, shiny car arrived outside the hotel at eight o'clock that evening. Lottie, Mrs Moore and Rosie were ready and waiting on the steps. Boris got out of the front passenger seat and explained that the prince was waiting for them on the steps of the casino.

'But we don't need a car,' Mrs Moore said to Boris. 'The casino is only across the road. It will take about twenty seconds to walk there!'

'You don't want to be seen arriving on foot,' said Boris. 'You must arrive in style.'

Stifling a laugh, Lottie climbed into the back of the car with Mrs Moore and cuddled Rosie on her lap. For her dress this evening, Mrs Moore had chosen a satin gown of ultramarine blue. She'd told Lottie she'd done so because it was the colour of the sea and Prince Manfred had a lot of interest in the sea.

Lottie's sequinned gown felt surprisingly comfortable. Mrs Moore had lent her long pink silk gloves, a necklace and a beaded headband with a sparkling silver leaf ornament.

The chauffeur pulled slowly away and encircled the oval of green in front of the casino twice.

'Golly, he's trying to make a journey of it,' said Mrs Moore.

Lottie couldn't resist a giggle.

About a minute later, the car pulled up outside the casino where Prince Manfred awaited them on a red carpet. He wore a striped jacket of purple and gold and an emerald green cravat and green trousers. His dark curls looked glossier and bouncier than ever.

'Mrs Moore!' He kissed her hand once she had alighted from the car. 'Allow me Monte Carlo Casino show you!'

'You've learned some English, Prince Manfred! How clever of you.'

He bowed and grinned in reply, and Lottie followed them up the red carpet and into the casino.

THE SHEER OPULENCE of the place almost hurt her eyes. Golden light glowed on every surface, from the sparkling crystals of the chandeliers to the ornate moulding on the walls and ceiling. Well-perfumed guests in smart evening wear gathered around the gaming tables, and Lottie felt she fitted in well in her gown.

The prince took Mrs Moore's arm and guided her to the roulette table.

'I'm not putting any money on anything,' Lottie heard her protest. 'I'll just watch you.'

Boris accompanied them, and soon they were lost in a small crowd around the table. Lottie remained with Rosie and decided to walk around and take in the splendour of the place. She was also interested in the private room where Mr Johnson had met his demise just two nights previously. It was difficult to believe something so dreadful had happened here.

She strolled through a couple of palatial rooms and eventually found what she was looking for: a velvet curtained doorway with a sign next to it saying "Salon Privé". Lottie felt a chill. Beyond the curtain was the room where Hector Johnson had been murdered. She didn't want to risk sneaking beyond the curtain, if she was found out then she'd be asked to leave and that could embarrass Mrs Moore and Prince Manfred. Instead, she continued looking around and taking everything in.

She caught sight of Beatrice sitting at a semi-circular table. Its green baize was marked out for a game which Lottie felt she had little hope of understanding. Beatrice examined some cards in her hand, then moved a stack of chips into position before taking a large swig from a glass of champagne.

Lottie moved on and wondered if Madame and Monsieur Rochefort were here this evening. If they were, then she would avoid them. She regretted calling on them earlier and felt sure they wouldn't be pleased to see her again.

Then she spotted a familiar dark-haired young man in a white suit and apron. She watched as he picked up a crystal glass ashtray from a table and replaced it with an empty one.

She approached him. 'Hello Henri.'

He politely bowed his head. 'How can I help? You know my name?'

'Yes, it's me, Lottie.'

'Lottie?' His mouth gaped. 'The girl with the corgi? Of course it's you! There's your dog!' He grinned. 'I didn't recognise you. You look completely different!'

She felt her face warm up. 'Thank you. My employer insisted I dress up for this evening. She's here with Prince Manfred of Bavaria.'

'The prince with the curly hair and the colourful clothes? I know who you mean. I didn't realise your employer knows him too.'

'She's hoping to marry him.'

'Is she? Well, he seems very... er...'

'Nice?'

'I suppose he is. And rich.'

'Did you manage to speak to any of your colleagues about the note in Mr Johnson's jacket?'

'Yes, I did.' He glanced down at the full ashtray in his hand. 'Just let me get rid of this and I'll tell you about it.'

Lottie waited as he disappeared behind a service door hidden in the ornate wainscoting and, a moment later, he was back. 'It's a mystery,' he said. 'I spoke to Louis, the doorman who you say has a large chin.'

'I didn't mean it unkindly.'

'I know that. It's funny. He does have a large chin. He says he didn't look in the jacket pockets, but he left the jacket in the cloakroom. Marianne, who works there, told me she looked in the pockets and found an empty wallet, an empty cigar case and a few other things. But there was no note.'

'How strange.' Lottie could only imagine that either Louis or Marianne was lying. But she didn't want to suggest this to Henri in case they were friends of his.

'Perhaps it fell out?' she suggested.

'Maybe. You'd think someone would have found it. I've discovered who the other people in the private room with Mr Johnson were. One of them is the Belgian racing car lady that you told me about.'

'Beatrice de Cambry de Baudimont.'

'Yes. And the French couple are Joseph and Marie Rochefort. They own the biggest department store in Paris. It was founded by Joseph Rochefort's grandfather and now he's in charge of it.'

'I met them earlier today.'

'You did?'

'Beatrice told me their name, and I managed to find them,

they're staying at the Hôtel Metropole. I asked them about Mr Johnson's jacket and... well, I'm embarrassed about it now. I foolishly asked them about him and obviously they said they had no idea who murdered him. I decided to do some detective work, but I think it was a mistake.'

'It was brave of you. What were they like?'

'I think they were a bit puzzled by my appearance and I don't blame them. They weren't very friendly and Monsieur Rochefort seemed keen to end the conversation, probably because he couldn't work out why I was there.'

'I don't suppose they're going to say much to a young woman they've never met before.'

'No. I think now that I shouldn't have tried to find them. Have you seen them here this evening?'

'No, but it's still early. They might turn up yet.'

'Do you know who the other poker player was that night?'

'An Englishwoman called Grace Harrison. But I've never seen her and I know nothing more about her.'

'So she's mysterious.'

'Very mysterious.'

'Mysterious enough to be the murderer, perhaps? If no one knows anything about her and she's now vanished, then she could have done it, couldn't she?'

'She could have. Perhaps she's here this evening? I wouldn't know because I wouldn't recognise her. I almost didn't recognise you!' He grinned.

'So how can I find Miss Harrison?' Lottie asked.

'You want to find her?'

'I want to know what she saw on the evening Mr Johnson was murdered.'

'You really are determined to be a detective, aren't you?'

'I am. I can't help it. Ever since I found that note, I've been thinking about it. Someone threatened Mr Johnson. And perhaps it was Miss Harrison? The note was written in English and you've told me she was English. Presumably Madame and Monsieur Rochefort would have written the note in French.'

'Not if it's for a person who only speaks English. Mr Johnson was American, wasn't he? I think if someone wanted to write to him, then they would do so in English.'

'I suppose they would. I know what I can do. I'll speak to Beatrice. She couldn't remember Miss Harrison's name, but she'll be able to give me a description of her. And perhaps Miss Harrison gave away some clues about herself during the evening.'

'It's worth a try.' He glanced about. 'There's no sign of my supervisor, so I've probably got a few more minutes before I get back to work. Do you want to see the room?'

'Where Mr Johnson was murdered?' Lottie felt a shiver run down her spine.

'Yes. The room's closed at the moment. No one will want to use it for some time. A lot of guests are quite superstitious and they wouldn't want to play cards in a room where bad luck has occurred.'

'That makes sense. Alright then. Let's have a look at it.'

Chapter Fifteen

'COME THIS WAY,' said Henri as he led Lottie and Rosie to the velvet curtain by the sign for the private rooms. He pushed the curtain aside, and they followed him into a dimly lit corridor with a thick carpet. They passed a couple of shiny doors before reaching one at the end of the corridor. He opened it and turned on the light. 'Here we are.'

Lottie peered in, unsure whether she actually wanted to step inside. A large oval table sat in the centre of the room, covered in blue baize cloth. Elegant mahogany chairs were placed around the table, and ornate lamps hung on the wall. A heavy, royal blue velvet curtain was pulled across the window.

'That's the curtain the murderer hid behind?' asked Lottie.

'Yes. And apparently Hector Johnson was found on the floor just there.' Henri pointed to a spot between the window and the door.

'It looks like a normal room.'

'Yes. It's not nice when you think about what happened here.'

Lottie stepped over to the blue curtain and felt the plush

velvet. There was little doubt it was thick and heavy enough to effectively conceal someone behind it. She moved the curtain aside and looked out of the window, it was close to sunset and not yet dark. The window offered a view of the side of the Cafe de Paris. People sat at the tables outside the cafe enjoying an evening drink.

Lottie replaced the curtain. 'How did the murderer know Hector Johnson was going to return to this room for his reading glasses?'

'They must have known he'd left them here.'

'That's very observant of them, wouldn't you say?'

'If they were planning to murder him, then they would have been watching his every move.'

'So they noticed he'd left his glasses behind and then hid behind the curtain and waited for him to return?'

'I think so,' said Henri.

'So the murderer must have been the last person to leave the room when the game had finished. They wouldn't have wanted anyone to see them hiding behind the curtain.'

'Not necessarily. They could have left the room but returned before Mr Johnson did.'

Lottie pondered over this. 'There are a lot of possibilities, aren't there? What about the dealer? Who was that?'

'That was Michel. He says he didn't see anything.'

'Would he have been the last person to leave this room after the game had finished?'

'Yes, I should think so. There would have been a few things to do, such as tidying up the cards.'

'So everyone left the room, but Mr Johnson left his spectacles here and had to return for them. Why didn't Michel the dealer spot the spectacles when he was tidying away the cards?'

'That's a very good point.'

'Maybe the murderer took the spectacles,' said Lottie, a new idea forming in her head. 'Perhaps they purposefully hid them so that Hector Johnson would have to return for them. I think they left the room with everyone else and waited for the dealer to leave. After the dealer left, they returned to the room and left the spectacles somewhere. Maybe on the table. Then they hid behind the curtain and waited for Mr Johnson to come in.' Then she thought some more. 'Perhaps they didn't even hide behind the curtain at all? They could have just waited here for Mr Johnson. Where did the idea they hid behind the curtain come from?'

'The rope tie is on a hook on the wall behind the curtain,' said Henri. 'So the murderer must have looked behind the curtain to find it. But you could be right, Lottie. Perhaps they didn't hide at all. I think they must have hidden so they could spring a surprise on him. If they'd confronted him, then he would have had a chance of fighting them off. But if someone's hiding, then they can jump out and launch a surprise attack on their victim. It's easier to overcome someone that way, isn't it?'

'I suppose it is. You sound like you know from experience.' She laughed.

'I definitely don't! It's just a guess.'

'I wonder what the motive was?'

'I don't think it was theft because Hector Johnson's winnings from that night were still in his pocket when he was found.'

'Really? So he was murdered for another reason then.'

'Perhaps you might learn more from Michel who was the dealer that night. He's working this evening and might have a break soon. I'll speak to him, then come and find you again.'

'Thank you.'

LOTTIE RETURNED to the main casino rooms and found Mrs Moore and Prince Manfred still at the roulette table. The prince had stacks of pink chips in front of him and Mrs Moore was clapping her hands with glee as the roulette wheel span around.

'Oh, no luck that time!' She sipped champagne as the croupier gathered in the chips. Then she put down her glass and excitedly distributed more chips for the next game. 'Number thirty-three again because that's my favourite. And I also want a split here and a street there. I think we need a corner too.'

The prince gave a chuckle. 'Now we win?' he asked.

'Yes, just watch!'

Lottie noticed Beatrice was at the table too. She had a look of fearsome concentration on her face and was giving Mrs Moore and the prince sidelong glances as she arranged her red chips in various positions.

The croupier spun the ball on the wheel and the table fell into hushed silence.

'Vingt-quatre,' he announced.

'What's that again?' asked Mrs Moore.

'Twenty-four,' muttered Beatrice as she watched the croupier remove her chips.

'Oh yes, we got something!' Mrs Moore clapped her hands again as the croupier removed some chips and passed her others. 'Oh, this is such a fun game!'

It wasn't long before Lottie felt a tap on her shoulder. She turned to see Henri with a grey-haired gentleman with large blue eyes. 'This is Michel Rossi,' said Henri. 'He's got about five minutes.'

They went back to the private room and Michel stood uncomfortably by the doorway. 'I don't want to be in this room for any longer than is necessary,' he said. 'What do you want to know?'

'Who was the last to leave the room?' asked Lottie.

'That was me.'

'And there was definitely no one else in here when you left?'

'No.'

'Did you see Mr Johnson's spectacles anywhere in here?'

'No. I remember he was wearing them when he was looking at his cards. He would put them on, then take them off again, and put them on again and so on. He rested them on the table, but I didn't see them here after he left.'

'Who was sitting where?' Lottie asked.

'Mr Johnson sat at this end,' said Michel. 'On his left was Madame Rochefort and on his right was Miss de Cambry de Baudimont. I was next to her and next to Madame Rochefort was her husband. At the end of the table was Miss Harrison.'

'Do you think one of the players could have taken Mr Johnson's spectacles and hidden them from him?'

'Why would they do that?'

'To make him think he'd lost them so he would come back to this room to find them.'

'Ah, I see! I suppose either Madame Rochefort or Miss de Cambry de Baudimont could have done that. I didn't see them do it, though.'

'Could Monsieur Rochefort or Miss Harrison have taken them?'

'They were both sitting farther away from Mr Johnson and I didn't see them do it. Perhaps one of them did it when they got up from the table, but it's impossible to say.'

'What was Miss Harrison like?'

'Young. English. Quite beautiful with dark hair which was short.' He gestured this with his hands by his ears. 'She didn't say much. She was quiet. Mr Johnson kept looking at her because I think they had an argument.'

'Really? When?'

'Before the game. I was on my way to the room to get it

ready and I saw them at the bar. He seemed to be talking to her angrily, and she appeared to be defending herself.'

'Have you seen her here at the casino since that night?'

'No.'

'I don't suppose she mentioned which hotel she was staying at?'

'No. Not that I remember.'

'Had you seen her here before?'

'Yes, she came in a few times and played in another game with Mr Johnson a few nights before.'

'Do you think she knew him well?'

'I don't know how well. But I think they knew each other. She didn't talk much the other evening, Mr Johnson did most of the talking. Some people, when they play poker, they like to be quiet because they're concentrating. Other people like to talk a lot, sometimes it's because of their nerves.'

A man appeared in the doorway and, judging by Henri and Michel's startled reaction, he was important. He had piercing green eyes, a grey moustache and wore a smart evening suit.

'What a surprise to find you here,' he said. Lottie wondered if he would have been angrier had she not been present. 'May I enquire why you are showing our guest this particular room?'

'Miss Sprigg asked to see the private rooms and the others are occupied, sir,' replied Henri.

'I see. You have explained to our guest that this room isn't currently available for use?'

'Yes, I've explained that. She just wanted an idea of what the rooms are like.'

He turned to the croupier. 'Michel, you're needed at your table.'

'Of course.'

'Thank you, gentlemen, for showing me the room,' Lottie

said. 'I'm sorry to have kept you from your work.' She turned to the grey, moustached man. 'And I apologise to you, sir, for distracting your staff. They've been extremely helpful.'

He gave a slight bow. 'I'm pleased to hear it. I'm Monsieur Blanchard, the casino manager. Do let me know if there is anything further we can assist you with.'

Lottie wanted to ask him all about Hector Johnson's murder, but he already seemed suspicious about why the three of them were in the room where Mr Johnson had been murdered. She decided not to pry any further for the time being.

They left the room, and she caught up with Michel before he went off to his table. 'Thank you very much, Michel, for talking to me. It's much appreciated.' He gave a nod and went on his way. As he departed, she caught the eye of someone familiar. A tall, beautiful lady dressed in black and gold.

It was Marie Rochefort.

The manner in which she looked at Lottie suggested she recognised her but couldn't quite place her. Lottie gave her a slight smile and left before Madame Rochefort remembered too clearly.

'Oh Lottie!' said Mrs Moore, holding her arm as they left the casino. 'I believe I helped the prince win five thousand francs! Although, that said, I probably helped him spend five thousand francs as well. I think he probably broke even. Which is better than losing, isn't it?' The manner in which she held onto Lottie's arm suggested she was a bit tipsy.

'What have you done with the prince now?'

'I've bid him goodnight. I've had more than enough now and I think he stays at the casino until four o'clock in the morning or something like that. He can carry on without me, although I think he'll miss my advice.'

'Do you think you'll be tempted to visit again?'

'Only if I spend someone else's money. I've no intention of ever parting with my own money in a place like that. You can't be too careful. Just as you convince yourself you're having a winning streak, it all goes horribly wrong. I wouldn't want to lose money in that way, I'd never forgive myself. Did you see Beatrice in there? It's quite easy to see how people get caught up in it, isn't it? After all, it's great fun. If there was a way of playing at those tables without spending any money, then I'd do it in a jiffy.'

'Isn't that what you managed this evening?'

'Yes, I suppose it was. How funny! Come on then, Lottie, let's get back to the hotel. I don't think there's any need for Prince Manfred's car to drive us back, do you?'

Chapter Sixteen

'MERCI.' Grace Harrison thanked the waiter and looked out again at the harbour. It was another beautiful sunny morning. She watched the bright white sail of a yacht diminish in size as the boat sailed out to sea. She wished she could be on that boat now, leaving Monaco behind and searching out new adventures. Where could she sail to? A Mediterranean island perhaps, she'd heard that Corsica was the nearest. Or could she sail to the northern coast of Africa? Apparently, it was less than 500 miles away.

She took a sip of her coffee, it was strong and bitter just as she liked it. What would the Monaco police do if she slipped away on a boat? Probably nothing. She wasn't enjoying being stuck here while the commissaire made his enquiries. She had liked Monaco when she'd first arrived, but having to stay here against her will was putting her off the place.

Her thoughts were disturbed by a throbbing engine noise and a shiny red car pulled up by the harbourside. She watched as a stocky figure in motoring overalls climbed out of the vehicle and strode towards the cafe. As the driving cap and goggles were removed, she realised the motorist was a lady. And someone she recognised.

She adjusted her sunglasses and lowered the brim of her sunhat. Hopefully the Belgian motoring lady would pass by without noticing her.

'Oh, hello!'

She had noticed her.

'Good morning.'

'We played poker together the other evening, didn't we? You'll have to remind me of your name again, I'm afraid.'

'Grace Harrison.'

'Beatrice de Cambry de Baudimont. Just call me Beatrice, though. I think I said that to you the other evening as well. Were you as hopeless at remembering my name as I was yours?'

'Yes.'

'What a pair we are!'

To Grace's horror, Beatrice took a seat at her table. Then she rested her cap and goggles on it and pulled off her driving gloves. She summoned a waiter and placed an order in French. Then she turned to Grace. 'Another coffee?'

'No, I'm fine, thank you. I'm just about to leave.'

'Where are you off to?'

'I'm going for a walk.'

'Ah, so nothing urgent then. I hope you'll stay here long enough for us to have a quick chat. Cigarette?'

'No, thank you.' Grace watched as Beatrice lit one for herself.

'What do you think about all this business with Hector Johnson?'

'I think it's awful.'

'Quite brazen, wasn't it? I don't know why someone chose that room to murder him in. Why not wait until he'd left the casino? It would have been much easier out on a dark street.'

'Or why do it at all?'

'There is that, I suppose. It's a bit unnecessary and is causing us all sorts of bother with the police breathing down our necks. Have you spoken to the commissaire?'

'Yes.'

'Me too. What did he ask you?'

'Probably the same things he asked you.'

'He seems a dozy sort, doesn't he? I can't imagine him catching the person who did it. It must have been that French couple, the Rocheforts, don't you think?'

'I don't know.'

'But surely you can't think it's me! Unless it's you?'

Grace shifted in her seat. She wasn't enjoying this conversation. 'I think it could have been anyone. Someone else could have walked in from the casino and hidden behind the curtain.'

'But it had to be someone who knew Mr Johnson had to go back for his reading glasses.'

'Oh yes.'

'Not many people would have known that, would they? Unless he told them. Perhaps he went out into the casino and then said to someone, "oh, I've got to get my reading glasses." Then off he went, and they followed him in there and murdered him.'

'That's a possibility.'

'I think it could be a good explanation.' Beatrice blew out a puff of smoke. 'And if that's the case, then the police need to be looking at everyone who was in the casino that evening and not just the people who played poker with Hector. We're stuck here, unable to leave, and yet it could have been someone who's travelled off elsewhere by now. It doesn't seem fair, does it?'

'It doesn't.'

A waiter arrived with Beatrice's coffee and she thanked

him before heaping several spoonfuls of sugar into it. 'I hope you don't mind me prying, Grace. But you and Mr Johnson seemed to know each other.'

She felt her stomach twinge. 'A little, we had met before.'

'Where?'

'Here in Monaco.'

'He seemed to be watching you a lot the other evening. In fact, he couldn't seem to keep his eyes off you. How well did you know him?'

'Not that well at all.' Grace felt her heart thudding in her chest. 'Do you mind if I have a cigarette?'

'Go ahead.' Beatrice held out the packet to her, and Grace didn't like her wry smile. Beatrice clearly realised she'd unearthed a secret and Grace had to be careful she let nothing else slip.

'How well did you know him?' Grace asked, determined to hit back.

'I didn't.' Beatrice flicked on her cigarette lighter and held it out for her. 'It was the first time I met him.'

Grace smiled to herself. It was quite obvious that Beatrice was lying too.

Chapter Seventeen

MRS MOORE WASN'T FEELING WELL ENOUGH to go down to the hotel restaurant for breakfast. 'I don't think I can eat anything,' she said, lying in bed.

'Perhaps you'd like to sit on your balcony and get a bit of sunshine? That might help.'

'I don't think I could cope with the brightness, Lottie. They're very good at serving you champagne in that casino. I don't think my glass was ever empty. Much as I tried to empty it, it kept refilling itself. It seemed to be a never-ending battle.'

'You appeared to have fun with Prince Manfred.'

'Oh, I did! And now I have to pay the price for it. Life can be quite unreasonable at times. Sometimes you feel you're being punished for having enjoyed yourself. Now you go along with Rosie and have some breakfast. I think I'll need to lie down in a darkened room for most of the morning.'

IN THE RESTAURANT, Lottie passed morsels of her breakfast to Rosie beneath the table and made some notes in her notebook. She drew a plan of the private casino room and noted where everyone had sat at the table.

And what about Michel Rossi? Was it possible the dealer could have murdered Hector Johnson? She only had Michel's word for it that he'd been the last to leave the room. Could he have taken Mr Johnson's glasses from him, then waited for him to return?

But if Michel had murdered Mr Johnson, what could his motive have been?

Robbery was ruled out. Had Mr Johnson been murdered because he'd been talkative and annoying? It didn't seem a strong enough reason.

The casino owner, Monsieur Blanchard, didn't seem likeable. He had a cold glint in his eye. Was it possible Mr Johnson had been causing a problem for the casino? Was he the sort of guest who won a lot in the casino and annoyed the manager? Had Mr Johnson cheated? If he'd upset Monsieur Blanchard in some way, then perhaps the manager had ordered Michel to murder him. Having met Michel, Lottie struggled to think of the mild-mannered, grey-haired man as being capable of such an act. And why risk the casino's reputation? If Mr Johnson had cheated, then surely he would have been asked to leave and forbidden to return. There was surely no need to resort to murder.

And how could the missing note be explained? If Monsieur Blanchard had written it, then that could be the reason why the note had been removed from Hector Johnson's jacket.

Lottie wondered if Mr Johnson had discussed the note with anyone else. Had he travelled to Monaco with a friend? Which hotel had he been staying at?

And where could she find the mysterious Grace Harrison?

She wrote all this down and was so distracted by it that her cup of tea went cold. The more she thought about the case, the more questions she had.

LOTTIE TOOK Rosie out for a walk along the seafront after breakfast. It was another sunny morning and the sea breeze felt refreshing on her face. Rosie investigated the repaired wall and greeted passers-by with a tail wag.

'Shall we walk down to the harbour, Rosie?' said Lottie. 'It's a lovely morning for it.'

On the harbour front, Lottie came across a familiar red motor car.

'That's the one Beatrice drives,' she said to her dog. 'She must be nearby.'

A moment later, she spotted her sitting at a table outside a cafe with a young woman wearing sunglasses and a sunhat.

'Hello!' Beatrice gave her a wave, so she went over to her. 'Beautiful morning, isn't it? The perfect day for drinking coffee in the sunshine. Will you join us?'

The young woman in sunglasses bit her lip. 'Actually, I have to get going.'

'Oh nonsense, Grace, you can stay for another. Lottie, this is Grace Harrison. We played poker the other evening.'

The mysterious Miss Harrison, Lottie had finally found her! She looked about twenty-five and wore a pale pink dress with a wide collar. She seemed restless, as if keen to make her escape.

'Lottie Sprigg is a travelling companion to a wealthy American heiress,' Beatrice explained to her. 'In fact, where is Mrs Moore this morning, Lottie?'

'She's having a rest. She's tired from the casino last night.'

'Completely wore herself out spending the prince's money, I expect!' She laughed. 'That's the very best way to have fun at a casino, gamble with someone else's money. I'm not surprised she's tired this morning. There was a lot of champagne being consumed at that roulette table. Some people struggle the morning after, but I find a good drive in the mountains clears my head. Sit down, Miss Sprigg, you're making the place look untidy. Coffee?'

'Thank you.'

Rosie greeted Miss Harrison, and the young woman smiled as she stroked her. 'What's her name?' she asked.

'Rosie.'

'That's a lovely name.'

'So you also played poker with Hector Johnson?' Lottie asked her. She hadn't expected the young woman's face to fall as much as it did.

'Yes,' said Beatrice, seemingly helping her out. 'We've been discussing it. Neither of us can work out exactly how or why he got himself murdered.'

Lottie sensed Miss Harrison didn't want to talk about it. It was understandable, but frustrating when she wanted to gauge the young woman's reaction to the tragic event. She also wanted to ask her about the argument she'd reportedly had with Hector Johnson before the poker game.

'How long have you been in Monaco for?' she asked her.

'Nearly a week. I should have left for home two days ago.'

'Where is home?'

'Hertfordshire.'

'I've never been, but I've heard it's nice. Have you travelled to Monaco alone?'

'Yes.'

'And there's no shame in that,' said Beatrice. 'The world is much easier for ladies to travel alone now. Grace's father left her some money and now she can do what she likes with it.'

'I really must go for my walk now,' said Miss Harrison. She stubbed out her cigarette and got to her feet. 'It was good to see you again Beatrice, and nice to meet you, Lottie.'

She walked off in the direction of the rock and Beatrice puffed on her cigarette.

'Grace is quite mysterious,' she said. 'I'm sure she and Hector Johnson knew each other well, but she won't say much about it. Why could that be?'

'She perhaps doesn't want to be associated too closely with someone who's been murdered. Perhaps she's worried people will suspect her?'

'They'll only suspect her if she had a reason for murdering him.'

'Perhaps she has a reason?'

'What a thought!' Beatrice grinned. 'That could explain why she's keeping quiet about him. However, she doesn't look particularly strong. How could she have overpowered him enough to strangle him with a curtain rope?'

Lottie recalled Henri's theory. 'If she'd pounced on him from behind the curtain, then he wouldn't have had time to react.'

'Yes, I can see that. Even so, it takes a lot of strength to do something like that. And I'm not speaking from experience if you're thinking of suspecting me!'

Lottie laughed this off and felt relieved to see Beatrice smiling, too.

'What did you make of Michel who was the dealer at the poker game?' Lottie asked her.

'Was that his name? I barely paid him any attention at all. I was too busy concentrating.'

'Do you think he could have been the murderer?'

'I don't see why a dealer would murder one of the casino's customers. How would he get away with that? But maybe he did, and he is getting away with it at the moment. I don't have an answer for that, I'm afraid. I suppose he could be a suspect, just like the rest of us. Hopefully, the sleepy commissaire has been interviewing him too. Grace made the useful point that just about anyone could have crept into that room before Mr Johnson went back to fetch his reading glasses. It doesn't necessarily have to be one of the people who played poker with him that evening. What the commissaire needs to find out is the reason Hector Johnson was murdered. Once he knows that, then the murderer should be easy to find.'

'What do you think the reason could be?'

'I've no idea! Perhaps the Rocheforts got annoyed because he won? Perhaps the casino got annoyed because he was winning too often? Or perhaps someone like me got annoyed because he talked too much? That last suggestion was a joke, by the way. Do you fancy a spin?'

'A what?'

'A spin in my car. I've got a spare hat and goggles.'

'No, I'm...'

'Oh come on! You'll enjoy it.'

Chapter Eighteen

MARIE ROCHEFORT MARCHED into the cafe and immediately spotted the two Marseille police detectives in the corner. She strode over to them and slammed her handbag onto the table.

'What have you got on your faces?' she snapped.

'Moustaches,' replied the older of the two, Brunelle. The younger one, Boyer, seemed too frightened to speak to her.

'False moustaches?'

'You told us we looked like policemen and had to blend in. So we altered our appearance.'

'No, you didn't. You just look like two policemen wearing false moustaches. It's ridiculous. Have you any idea how much trouble you've caused?'

'Trouble?'

She sat down and lowered her voice. 'You do realise the Monaco police have spotted you here?'

'Yes.' Brunelle adjusted his moustache. 'They had a word with us and we told them we're watching Philippe Albertini.'

'The Monaco police have now told my husband that. And what do you suppose he's going to do?'

'Erm, well... it would be unfortunate if he were to tell Albertini.'

'It would be, wouldn't it?'

'Do you think you'll be able to dissuade him?'

'Dissuade him? How? For all I know, he's told him already.'

She watched the detective's face fall.

'Do you think he has told him?'

'I don't know! But if he has, you only have yourselves to blame. I told the pair of you that you looked too obvious. I think you failed to realise how small Monaco is. The police know everybody here and they're obviously going to spot undercover detectives. You should have made more of an effort. Perhaps you could have pretended to be rich tourists?'

'Rich?' said Boyer. 'We only get five francs for expenses each day.'

She sighed, struggling to believe how amateur they were. 'Perhaps you should have thought imaginatively then. Perhaps you could employ some women to do the job? I'm sure the police here in Monaco would never have suspected two women like they suspect you.'

'Women?' said Brunelle.

'There are plenty of women about with the skills, they learned them during the war.'

'We don't employ women.'

'Then perhaps you should try.'

She crossed her legs and lit a cigarette. The situation worried her. 'What about my deal?' she said. 'I agreed with the police in Paris that if I cooperate fully, then I can start a new life while my husband is locked up in prison.'

'I suppose that can still happen,' said Brunelle.

'How? If Albertini runs off and you have no evidence he and my husband colluded together on a crime, then you can't arrest them, can you? This is all a dreadful mess! And to think I spent so long trying to ensure it would work out!'

She adopted a wounded expression and allowed a silence to fall, hoping the detectives would use the opportunity to reflect on their ineptitude. Then she decided on a new approach.

'It pains me to say this,' she whispered. The two detectives leaned in, keen to hear her words. 'I think my husband may have... oh, it doesn't seem right to say it.'

'Say what?' asked Brunelle, his eyes wide with interest.

'It's the ultimate betrayal. I couldn't consider it.'

'Consider what?'

'Oh, very well. I haven't mentioned this to the Monaco police yet because... it's been hard enough even admitting it to myself! The murder of the American businessman, Hector Johnson. You've heard about it?'

'Yes. We read about in the newspaper.'

'Well, I think the Monaco police need all the help they can get, you should volunteer your services.'

'Our department wouldn't allow that, Madame Rochefort.'

'Your department doesn't need to know, does it? And imagine what high regard you'll be held in when you return to Marseille having solved a murder.'

'Solved it? How?'

'Have you met Commissaire Verrando?'

'No.'

'He's close to retirement and can't really be bothered with the case.'

'That's not very professional.'

'It's not, is it? He has men to help him, but when the leadership is poor, everything flounders, doesn't it? Now imagine that two shrewd detectives from Marseille happen to be in town and solve the case under his nose. Wouldn't that be something?'

Brunelle's mouth lifted into a faint smile.

'I can tell you'd like that, wouldn't you?'

'Possibly.' His face grew serious again. 'But we're not the investigating detectives, there's not a lot we can do.'

'Oh, there is. Especially when you have some information.'

'What information?'

'My husband disappeared on the night of Mr Johnson's death.'

'Disappeared?'

'Not for long. But for half an hour, I had no idea where he'd got to. That half hour was around the time Mr Johnson was murdered. The thought is unthinkable but... I had to share it with someone. And the commissaire is inept and probably wouldn't listen to me, anyway. So all I can do is tell you about it and hope that... well, I'll let you decide how you wish to proceed.'

She squashed her cigarette into the ashtray, got to her feet and picked up her handbag.

'Just think of the rewards, gentlemen, if you can solve this.'

She turned and left before they could respond.

Chapter Nineteen

LOTTIE HADN'T TRAVELLED in a sporty motor car before and Beatrice was persuasive. Eventually, Lottie agreed to go with her.

'You won't drive fast, will you?' she asked as they walked towards the red Bugatti.

'There's no fun in driving slowly.'

'But please, not very fast.'

Beatrice laughed. 'Alright then.' She reached into the car, pulled out a hat and goggles and handed them to Lottie. 'Have you been in one of these things before?'

'No.'

'You'll never want to ride in anything else again.'

'Will I not?'

Beatrice opened the passenger door and Lottie climbed in. The leather seat was low, and it felt as though she was sitting only a few inches above the ground. She pulled on the hat and goggles, then lifted Rosie onto her lap. The roof of the car was folded down and there was only a small glass windshield in front of them. Lottie imagined it would be quite breezy once they got moving.

Beatrice strode to the front of the vehicle and turned the crank. The engine rattled into life and the entire car shuddered. Rosie gave Lottie a look of alarm.

'It's alright,' she said to her. 'I think you'll enjoy it once we get going.'

Beatrice climbed into the seat next to her. 'Are you ready?' she shouted over the engine.

'Yes,' replied Lottie. But her voice was barely audible above the noise.

Beatrice deftly moved some levers, then they were off. The swift movement pushed Lottie back into her seat. It was quite a thrilling sensation.

The car picked up speed and they took the road up from the harbour towards the hotel and casino. This was the road which Lottie and Mrs Moore had first seen Beatrice zooming along. To Lottie's relief, Beatrice wasn't driving as fast as she had on that occasion. She was still travelling at a good speed though, and they were quickly past the hotel, through the Place du Casino and up a street lined with attractive hotels and shops. The noise of the car's engine attracted a few glances from pedestrians, and Lottie sensed Beatrice enjoyed the attention.

Rosie's tongue lolled out of her mouth and she edged closer to the door so she could peer out over it. Lottie clung on to her as firmly as she could without hurting her.

The road curved to the left, then Beatrice took a sharp right and propelled the car up another street. After another sharp turn, the streets narrowed and there was only enough space for one vehicle to pass through at a time. Beatrice clearly expected everyone else to get out of her way as they sped past delivery vans, motorbikes and pedestrians. She powered up a narrow street which ended in a steep flight of steps. Lottie was wondering how the car was going to climb them when Beatrice turned sharply to the left, and Lottie and Rosie were flung against the door.

Having begun the journey quite sensibly, Beatrice was speeding up. The breeze whipped at Lottie's face. She held onto Rosie and hoped the journey wouldn't take long. She wished she'd agreed on a length of time with Beatrice before getting into the car.

'We're in France now!' Beatrice shouted. 'We've crossed the border!'

She swung the car into a sharp right bend and the buildings dropped away as they sped up the next hill. Lottie could see over the rooftops of Monaco now, and the Mediterranean glistened beyond. Above them, the mountains loomed closer. Lottie wondered how far into France Beatrice was planning to go.

The road zig-zagged up the mountain. Rocks and scrub lined one side while a precipitous drop lay on the other. Lottie wasn't keen on the speed at which Beatrice took the hairpin bends. Just one slight mistake with the steering wheel could send them tumbling over the edge.

Lottie gritted her teeth and had to remind herself to breathe. She also reminded herself that Beatrice was an experienced driver and was in full control of the car.

Rosie was enjoying the ride, and the breeze blew her tongue to one side of her mouth. Lottie laughed and tried to relax a little and enjoy the drive. She felt a twinge of exhilaration from the powerful engine. This was an experience she was looking forward to telling Mrs Moore about when she returned to the hotel.

Eventually the road levelled out and, after a few more sharp bends, they arrived in a small village. The roar of the car engine disturbed its peace.

'There's a nice little viewpoint up here,' shouted Beatrice

as she hurled the car down a narrow track. They bumped along it until she came to a sudden halt.

Beatrice turned off the engine, then pulled off her hat and goggles. 'We'll need to walk the last bit, which is a shame. I don't like walking.'

LOTTIE PEELED off her own hat and goggles, then opened her door. Rosie jumped off her lap and began exploring the wooded track. They followed Beatrice, who was already marching off to the viewpoint. After twenty yards, the trees parted, and the blue sky and aquamarine sea greeted them. Monaco glimmered beneath them. Lottie could see the Rock of Monaco and could just make out the fortified walls of the Prince's Palace on it. The sun was warm, and birdsong came from the scrubby little trees around them.

'Beautiful, isn't it?' said Beatrice, surveying the scene with her hands on her hips. 'The French Riviera! That's Cape Martin over there.' She pointed to her left. 'I think you can see Menton too. And beyond that lies Italy.' She pointed to the right. 'Nice is in that direction. Have you been to Nice?'

'No,' said Lottie.

'You should. It's nice,' Beatrice laughed. 'Let's get back in the car!'

LOTTIE FELT a sense of trepidation as she sat in the passenger seat and pulled on her hat and goggles again. She hadn't enjoyed the hairpin bends on the climb up here. What were they going to be like on the way down?

Chapter Twenty

BEATRICE STEERED the car through the village, then took off down the first downhill stretch of road. Lottie watched as the sharp bend at the end loomed closer, then screwed her eyes shut as Beatrice swung the car to the left. Lottie and Rosie lurched to the right, then the car straightened, and they hurtled towards the next bend.

'Oh, hello!' shouted Beatrice. 'Looks like we've got a friend!'

'Where?'

'Behind us!'

Lottie turned to see a black car with large, round head-lamps. The driver hunched over the wheel and wore a black driving cap and goggles.

Beatrice swung the car around the next bend and the car behind slowed as it followed. On the next stretch of road, however, it caught up with them.

'A Bentley 3 Litre Tourer,' said Beatrice, glancing into the little mirror attached to the side of the windshield. 'Faster than this car, but bigger and heavier. Why's he driving so close behind?'

They took the next bend so sharply that Lottie felt sure the car was going to roll over the low wall which separated the road from the rocky drop. Once again, the Bentley was slower on the corner. But on the next stretch, it overtook.

'Who is that?' shouted Beatrice. 'And why are they in such a hurry?'

The black Bentley slowed at the next bend and Beatrice pushed the nose of her car dangerously close behind it. Lottie stared at the spare wheel strapped to the back and gritted her teeth, bracing herself for a collision.

'Out of my way!' shouted Beatrice. She sounded her horn.

The Bentley slowed even more on the next straight stretch.

'What's he doing?' Beatrice swung the car to the left and powered on past, overtaking the Bentley but heading straight for a van which was climbing the road in the opposite direction. Lottie's heart jumped into her mouth.

'Whoops!' yelled Beatrice, swinging the car back in at the last minute. The van honked its horn at them but the sound was soon lost as they sped on round the next corner, the rear of the car drifted and pulled them closer to the edge of the road. Beatrice spun the steering wheel, and Lottie clutched Rosie with her right arm while clinging to the seat with her left hand. Her mouth was dry.

'He's back behind us again!' shouted Beatrice. 'Does he want a race? I'll show him a race!'

'Can't we just stop?' cried out Lottie, but Beatrice didn't seem to hear.

The Bugatti raced onwards, and the tyres squealed on the next bend. Once again, Lottie heard an engine close behind and she turned to see the Bentley's headlamps just inches from the back of the car. She was flung against the door on the next bend and the Bentley tore past on the straight section.

'He's going to cause an accident!' yelled Beatrice. The Bentley slowed in front of them, but this time it weaved right and left as Beatrice attempted to pass. 'What's he playing at? Is he trying to force us to stop?'

As the next bend approached, Beatrice turned before they reached it and bumped the car over the dirt and gravel on the corner. For a terrifying moment, they were heading straight for the low wall at the side of the road. But Beatrice managed to turn in time to straighten the car on the road.

The Bentley driver seemed unimpressed with this. He pulled up alongside them, then edged his vehicle closer. It was almost twice the size of Beatrice's car, and Lottie felt sure it could nudge them off the road quite easily. She could see the driver clearly now. A clean-shaven man, his head and eyes covered.

'We need to stop!' she shouted. The edge of the road and the steep drop was only inches from where she sat. She didn't know whether to cry or scream. Nausea lurched in her stomach.

Beatrice steered towards the Bentley, as if refusing to be intimidated. Lottie held her breath as the cars almost touched. Surely there was going to be a terrible accident?

Then another car appeared on the opposite side of the road. The Bentley braked sharply and moved in behind Beatrice. They remained in front as they rounded the next corner. They were almost back in the town. Surely the chase couldn't continue there?

With an engine roar, the Bentley drew alongside again. Beatrice wisely slowed so he couldn't nudge the Bugatti and the Bentley was once more in front of them. Another game of weaving ensued and there was no getting past the black car. Then the Bentley braked sharply, and Lottie felt sure they were going to crash into the back of it. Beatrice's reactions were quick. She swung the Bugatti out and around the Bentley and sped on past.

The next bend brought them into the town. A man

crossing the road leapt out of the way as Beatrice sped towards him.

Lottie closed her eyes. She couldn't bear this anymore.

But the car slowed and Lottie turned to see the Bentley stopped at the bend behind them.

She breathed out an enormous sigh. 'He's given up!' she cried.

Chapter Twenty-One

'WHAT NOW?' Joseph Rochefort stood in Commissaire Verrando's office with his hands on his hips.

'Please take a seat, Monsieur Rochefort.'

'I haven't got time, I need this to be quick.'

The commissaire adjusted his glasses. 'Please take a seat, Monsieur Rochefort. What I am about to tell you is of a sensitive nature.'

Joseph groaned. 'What?'

'Please sit and I shall tell you.'

Joseph slumped into the chair irritated that he was now sitting lower than the detective.

The commissaire leafed through the papers on his desk, then handed a small piece of paper to Joseph. It was folded in half. Joseph opened it out and saw it was a note. It was written in English and was addressed to Hector Johnson. He recognised the handwriting, it belonged to his wife.

Joseph handed the note back to the commissaire. 'Why are you showing me this?'

'Have you read it?'

'Yes, but it's in English, so I don't understand every word. My wife's English is better than mine.'

'Do you want me to translate it for you?'

'There's no need.'

'I think it's quite important that you understand what the note says.'

'I think I know what the note says. I'm fully aware my wife and Hector Johnson were conducting an affair. Well, it wasn't much of an affair because he was in America and she was in France. But I know it was something which was rekindled when he was in this country.'

'Did the affair anger you?'

'No. Because it wasn't much of an affair. And if you think I murdered Hector Johnson because he was in love with my wife, then you're quite wrong.'

To Joseph's pleasure, the commissaire seemed a little deflated. The detective had clearly thought he'd come across an important lead. But all he'd found was some paltry note his wife had written to her lover.

'Is there anything else?' asked Joseph.

Commissaire Verrando looked through the papers on his desk again. 'No, I think that was all. Oh, have you seen Philippe Albertini recently?'

'No, I'm staying away from him on your advice. I had no idea the man was a criminal, so I'm having nothing else to do with him.'

'Very wise.'

'There's something I'd like to mention to you before I go, actually.'

'Yes?'

'There's an English girl who's behaving a little... strangely.'

The commissaire furrowed his brow. 'In what way?'

'She turned up unannounced at our hotel with her dog

and began asking me and my wife questions about Mr Johnson's jacket.'

'She's still talking about that, then.'

'She mentioned it to you?'

'Yes, she did.'

'I don't understand what that's about. But there was another odd thing, too. My wife saw her at the casino last night.'

'Why's that unusual?'

'It's not unusual in itself. But she wasn't doing the usual things. My wife didn't see her at any of the tables or socialising with anyone there other than two members of staff.'

'Who were the members of staff?'

'One was a young lad who tidies up after people, I couldn't tell you his name. I don't know it. But the other man was the dealer at the game of poker on the night that Johnson was murdered. And, what's more, my wife saw her and the two men appear from the corridor which leads to the private rooms. Perhaps they went to the scene of the crime? I suspect the English girl is nosing about.'

'Nosing about?'

'Yes. She wants information. I don't know why. Perhaps she was a friend of Mr Johnson's? Maybe she's even working for the French police?'

'Why would she be working for them?'

'I don't know. You told me there were French police here following Albertini about. Perhaps she's up to something similar? I thought I'd let you know about it because I find her behaviour strange.'

The commissaire picked up his pen and made a note in his notebook. 'Thank you Monsieur Rochefort, leave it with me.'

. . .

JOSEPH MET his wife at a table outside the Cafe de Paris and gave her a kiss on the cheek. She wore a lemon-coloured sunhat and matching dress.

'How's your morning been?' he asked her.

'Lovely. I went for a little walk by the harbour.'

'Very nice.' He snapped his fingers at a waiter and ordered coffee.

'How was the commissaire?' she asked.

'He wasted my time again with more pointless questions.' There was no use in him confronting her about the note. If he did so, then she'd mention his own infidelities and he didn't want those brought up while he was enjoying a coffee in sunny Monte Carlo.

'I told him about the English girl, though.'

'Good. Although I shouldn't think he'll do anything.'

'Who do you think she is? Do you think she's been sent here to watch me?'

'Watch you? Why you?'

'I don't know. But ever since I heard about those undercover French policemen, I've been feeling wary. Perhaps we're being watched now?'

'Don't be silly, of course we're not.'

He glanced around at the other tables. As he did so, a man at a table behind him raised his newspaper so it covered his face.

His breath felt shallow. Was there no place to hide?

Then his eyes were drawn to the black Bentley which was pulling up outside the casino.

'Look who it is,' said Marie.

Joseph got up from his seat. 'I'll go and speak to him.'

Chapter Twenty-Two

LOTTIE'S LEGS felt weak as she staggered out of Beatrice's Bugatti outside the Hôtel de Paris. She cuddled Rosie close to her chest. Remarkably, the corgi seemed quite content.

'Well, that was a bit of fun, wasn't it?' said Beatrice.

'*Fun*?' Lottie couldn't believe how unbothered she was. 'I thought we were going to crash!'

'Not with me at the wheel we weren't!' She patted Lottie on the arm. 'Come along, let's find you a stiff drink. Gin and lime?'

'I don't want a stiff drink. I just want a lie down.'

'Alright then. You go and recover yourself.'

'Who was driving that other car?'

'I've no idea.'

'Why was he driving like that?'

'I think he was trying to stop us. But he learned the hard way, there's no stopping me!'

'But why did he want us to stop?'

'Who knows? If we see him around, we can ask him. Why don't you get your rest now and I'll see you later.'

'I would thank you for the drive, but I'm afraid I didn't enjoy it very much.' Lottie could feel herself still trembling.

Beatrice laughed. 'The main thing is that you and Rosie are still in one piece.'

FIVE MINUTES after Lottie had laid down on her bed, Mrs Moore knocked on her door.

'Well, I feel nicely refreshed now, Lottie. Do you fancy a walk? Oh dear, you look rather pale. Are you coming down with something?'

As Lottie told her about the extraordinary drive with Beatrice, Mrs Moore's eyes widened.

'Good golly!' she said once Lottie had finished. 'It's a wonder you weren't driven off the road, just think what could have happened! You'd have tumbled down and down and—'

'I don't really want to think about it anymore.'

'No, of course not. Well, if it had been me, then I would have certainly died of fright. I don't know how you lived to tell the tale. And to be honest with you, I'm surprised you got in the car with her after having witnessed the way she drives about the place.'

'It was fine until that other car appeared. She drove fairly fast, but I was enjoying it. Then, for some reason, that man started driving at us as if he was... attacking us! I don't understand it.'

'Did Beatrice annoy him in some way? Sometimes motorists can get very angry if someone else is driving inconsiderately.'

'I don't think she did. The first I knew about the Bentley, it was driving right behind us. I think he wanted us to stop. I wish Beatrice had stopped so we could have found out what he wanted. But I think she thought it was some sort of competition or race, so she carried on.'

'Well, it sounds like a scary experience, but I'm relieved you and Rosie are safe now. I'll leave you in peace, but I'll be in the lounge if you need me.' She rested her hand on Lottie's and gave it a squeeze. 'I'm pleased you're back here safely. I would have been worried stupid if I'd known about you getting in that car!'

After Mrs Moore left, Lottie thought about the view she'd had of the Bentley driver's face. Did she recognise him? There had seemed something familiar about him, but she'd only seen the lower portion of his face.

And why had he wanted them to stop? Perhaps Mrs Moore was right, and Beatrice's driving had angered him. It didn't excuse him from driving dangerously though.

Perhaps the driver of the Bentley had been after Beatrice for another reason? Perhaps they'd encountered each other previously and had a falling out. Beatrice hadn't owned up to knowing him though, and she hadn't claimed to have recognised the car.

Then another thought came to Lottie, which gave her a chill. Perhaps the driver of the Bentley had been after her?

'I'M relieved you have a little colour in your cheeks now, Lottie,' said Mrs Moore at dinner that evening. 'I was worried about you earlier. It's good to see you have an appetite too.'

Lottie dipped a chunk of fresh crusty bread into her bouillabaisse fish stew and savoured the delicious flavours. She felt much more recovered now.

'Just wait until I see that Beatrice lady,' said Mrs Moore. 'I'm going to have serious words with her about scaring you like that.'

'Please don't, I'm sure there's no need.'

'I didn't enjoy seeing you all shaken up like that!'

'But I'm fine now, Mrs Moore. I really don't want a fuss to be made.'

'But what about Rosie? She must have been enormously frightened!' Lottie looked down at the corgi, who sat patiently by her chair waiting for a tasty morsel or two.

'Rosie's fine. In fact, she didn't seem scared at all. I think she enjoyed it!'

Mrs Moore shook her head. 'Well, if you insist everything is alright now, then I won't bring it up again. Just say no next time she asks you to get into her car.'

'I will.'

A waiter approached and handed Mrs Moore an envelope.

'Oh, how exciting! I expect this is from Prince Manfred. I hope it's not another invitation to the casino. I've only just recovered from last night.' She ripped open the envelope and read the message inside. 'We're invited on a boat trip with him tomorrow! It says here that he's invited a group of friends. That's a little disappointing. It won't be just me and him. Although I suppose we always need Boris the interpreter with us too. I don't mind that at all, I've grown quite fond of Boris. He speaks five languages. English, German, Italian, Spanish and... oh, that's four. What's the other one? Oh, French, of course!' She smiled at the waiter, who remained standing at their table. 'What is it?' she asked him.

'The prince would like a reply.'

'Would he?'

'Yes, his messenger is waiting in the lobby.'

'Oh! I see now, it's written at the bottom here. "Répondez s'il vous plaît". He didn't put that on the last one. Even I know what that means!' She laughed.

'What would you like your reply to be, madam?' asked the waiter.

'Please tell the prince that I would be delighted to attend. And I shall bring my assistant and dog with me too. I don't want any harm coming to Lottie while I'm out enjoying myself on the high seas.'

'Very well.' The waiter gave a bow. Then his attention was distracted by a familiar rumble behind the window.

'Oh, it's Beatrice in that noisy motor car again,' said Mrs Moore as the red Bugatti pulled up outside the hotel. 'But don't worry, Lottie, I shan't embarrass you by telling her off.' She turned to the waiter. 'Doesn't the noise of that car get on your nerves?'

He gave a polite smile. 'We enjoyed our quiet day last week when the car was being repaired.'

'She had to have it repaired? I'm not surprised. She drives it so often that I suppose she must wear the engine out.'

The waiter gave another bow. 'I shall inform the prince's messenger of your response.'

'Thank you so much! Oh, how exciting, Lottie, a boat trip with the prince! We need to be at the harbour for eleven o'clock tomorrow.'

Chapter Twenty-Three

'ANOTHER GLORIOUS DAY,' said Mrs Moore as she surveyed the harbour through her lorgnette. She stood on the jetty with Lottie and Rosie and wore an enormous sun hat and a cream-coloured dress with a buttoned bodice and cuffs. 'That said, I can see a few clouds over there. I believe they're the first clouds we've seen since arriving here. Now, which boat do you think the prince is on?' She trained her lorgnette on the boats moored out in the harbour.

Lottie noticed a little motorboat making its way towards the jetty. 'Is that Boris?' she said.

'Yes!' said Mrs Moore. 'I'd recognise his blue suit anywhere. This must be the little launch to take us to the boat. How exciting!'

Moments later, the launch arrived and Boris jumped up onto the jetty, rope in hand, and greeted them with a bow. 'Mrs Moore! Miss Sprigg!' He tied the rope to a cleat on the jetty and gestured to the little boat where a grey-bearded man dressed in white held out his hand to help them on board. Lottie picked up Rosie and watched as Mrs Moore tentatively stepped in.

'Oh, I'm no good at this part,' she said. 'I've been known to fall at times like this.'

Boris applauded as soon as she was safely seated. 'Well done, Mrs Moore!'

Lottie followed her employer into the launch and sat on a little cushioned seat next to her.

'Where's the other lady?' asked Boris.

'Other lady?' said Mrs Moore.

'Yes. Ah, here she is!'

Lottie turned to see a young woman walking along the jetty. She wore a chic, caramel dress with matching hat, shoes and bag.

Lottie recognised her.

The young woman slowed her step as she noticed Lottie and Mrs Moore in the boat.

'Come aboard!' said Boris cheerily.

Lottie whispered to her employer. 'It's Grace Harrison. She was one of the poker players when Mr Johnson was murdered.'

Mrs Moore's eyes widened. 'What's she doing here?' she whispered back.

'I don't know.'

'Hello.' Miss Harrison forced a smile as she climbed into the boat with Mrs Moore and Lottie. 'I wasn't expecting other guests.'

'What a surprise for you, then,' said Mrs Moore sharply.

'Are we ready?' asked Boris.

'As ready as we'll ever be.'

'Off we go!' He untied the rope, jumped into the boat and they were off. Lottie cuddled Rosie on her lap and enjoyed the cooling sea spray on her face. The harbour quickly receded as they motored to the prince's boat.

After introducing herself to Miss Harrison, Mrs Moore

was quick with her next question. 'How do you know the prince?'

'I met him at the casino.'

'So you've not known him long, then?'

'No, just a few days.'

'Interesting.'

'Have you known him long?' asked Miss Harrison.

'Yes. I travelled here to Monaco with him.'

'How nice.'

'Yes. And before then we were in Cairo, Paris and Venice.'

'Goodness, you've travelled a lot.' She turned to Lottie. 'And we met yesterday, didn't we?'

'That's right. You were having coffee with Beatrice de Cambry de Baudimont.'

'Yes. Funny how we've bumped into each other twice now, isn't it?'

'Hilarious,' said Mrs Moore.

'I suppose it's because Monaco is so small,' continued Miss Harrison.

'That's probably something to do with it,' said Mrs Moore. It was clear from her curt responses that Mrs Moore felt resentful about Miss Harrison being invited along.

Soon they reached a gleaming white boat with a polished timber cabin. The launch pulled up alongside it, and Prince Manfred waved at them from the deck. Lottie had to stifle a giggle when she saw he was dressed as a sailor in white trousers and a smock top with a wide navy collar and knotted scarf.

A four-foot rope ladder led from the launch to the boat. Boris held it and gestured for Mrs Moore to climb.

'Oh. Right. Well, I'll give it a go.'

She stood up in the boat and held out her arms to steady herself. Lottie felt nervous for her, recalling her fall into a Venice canal and her topple from a camel in Egypt.

As both boats bobbed on the water, the gap between them widened and narrowed.

'You can do it!' encouraged Boris. Prince Manfred joined in with some clapping, which did little to help.

Wake from a passing vessel made the boats bob about even more and Mrs Moore lost her nerve. 'Oh no I can't.'

'Yes you can!' said Boris.

'It would be easier if there was a gangplank or something from dry land. But I'm afraid I'm not going to get on with this little ladder at all.'

Prince Manfred called down to Boris, and the interpreter invited Miss Harrison to board.

'Alright then.' She handed him her handbag and deftly climbed the ladder before leaning over and retrieving her bag from him.

'Miss Sprigg?' said Boris. 'We can put your dog on first.' Lottie handed Rosie to Boris, who then handed her up to Prince Manfred. He grinned and gave the dog a cuddle before placing her down on the deck.

The urge to be with Rosie encouraged Lottie to climb the ladder, and she found it surprisingly straightforward. Soon she was on the deck with Rosie and Prince Manfred, looking down at Mrs Moore in the launch.

'It's easier than it looks, Mrs Moore,' said Lottie.

Her employer still stood with her arms outstretched for balance. 'And it's easier to say that than actually do it. What if I fall into the gap between the boats?'

'You won't,' said Boris.

'You didn't see what happened to me in Venice!'

'Would it be easier if we didn't watch you?' asked Lottie.

'Yes! It would be much easier if no one watched me!'

Boris informed Prince Manfred of this and they moved down the deck, away from the rope ladder. There were about a dozen other people on board, some speaking in French and members of the prince's entourage speaking in German. Lottie moved past them to the bow of the boat and looked out over the harbour as she waited for her employer. The clouds which Mrs Moore had spotted earlier were gathering on the mountain range behind Monaco, casting their shadows on the hillside.

Miss Harrison stood close by, also looking out at the view.

'Have you been to Monaco before?' Lottie asked her.

'No, this is the first time.'

'And what do you make of it?'

'It's an interesting place. It has some lovely hotels and I like the casino. I like walking along the beach too. Have you been to the beach?'

'Not yet.'

Rosie trotted over to Miss Harrison and sniffed her fancy shoes. Miss Harrison bent down and patted the dog. 'My grandmother had a corgi.'

'Did she?'

'She was called Daphne. Your dog looks quite like her, actually. She's called Rosie, isn't she?'

'That's right. She's Italian.'

'Is she?'

'I adopted her in Venice.'

'In Venice! So she's used to boats and the water then.'

'Yes, she's quite accustomed to them.'

'She's very friendly, isn't she?'

'She loves people.'

'I can tell.' Miss Harrison patted Rosie some more and Lottie felt grateful for her pet's ability to break the tension with people she didn't know well.

'Here I am!' chimed a voice behind them.

Lottie turned to see Mrs Moore and was relieved to see she wasn't wet. 'You made it!'

'Yes, I made it. It's actually easier to climb up the ladder than it looks.'

'Is it?' Lottie pretended to sound surprised, and Mrs Moore laughed.

The boat's engine started up and there was lively chatter among the guests as they headed out to sea.

BORIS ASKED everyone to gather together so they could hear from the prince. Everyone listened as Prince Manfred delivered one of his speeches, which was translated by Boris.

'Thank you to you all, my gracious guests, for joining me on board this wonderful boat, Belle Reine. I hope you enjoy our little trip today. The skipper tells me that a change in the weather has been forecast, which means we cannot travel as far as I would have liked today. Unfortunately, we shall have to return to port sooner than we originally anticipated. However, we still have a few hours of fun ahead of us, so please relax and enjoy yourselves!'

This was met with a round of applause.

The boat headed for the stretch of water beyond the Rock of Monaco. Lottie glanced over at the clouds, which now had a tinge of grey about them. As they rounded the headland, Lottie's eye was drawn to a beautiful, classically styled building. Its lower storeys were built into the cliff face, giving it the appearance of having grown out of the rock.

'That's the Oceanographic Institute,' said Mrs Moore. 'The place Prince Manfred dragged me round the other day.' Then she lowered her voice to a hushed tone. 'I don't understand what Grace Harrison is doing here. I haven't seen her speak to the prince yet. And would he really invite her after meeting her in the casino? It all sounds rather strange to me. And what's a young English woman like her doing alone here in Monaco? Where is her money from?'

'Beatrice told me she has a wealthy father.'

'Well, if that's the case, surely he could have provided her with a chaperone? I realise it's old-fashioned to say such things these days, but I think a young woman has to be careful when travelling alone. And besides, it's quite boring isn't it? Everybody needs a trusty travelling companion to keep them company, wouldn't you agree?'

'Yes, I do.'

'Has she explained to you why the prince invited her here?'

'No. Although I'm more interested in what she can tell me about the evening she played poker with Hector Johnson.'

'Yes, that is interesting. I'd like to hear more about that too. But do you think she'd tell us? She seems a quiet sort. Secretive even. What's she hiding?'

Chapter Twenty-Four

CHAMPAGNE WAS SERVED, and Rosie visited each of the guests on the boat. Lottie kept a close eye on her, not wishing to lose her overboard. A breeze was picking up, and the sun was disappearing intermittently behind the clouds. Lottie hoped the captain would think about turning round soon.

If he did decide soon, then she wouldn't have much time to speak to Grace Harrison about Hector Johnson's murder. She decided to make the most of the opportunity she had and found Miss Harrison at the stern of the boat, speaking to Boris, the interpreter. Rosie greeted them which allowed Lottie into the conversation.

'We were just talking about sausages, Miss Sprigg,' said Boris. 'I understand you have sausages in England?'

'Yes.'

'In Bavaria, we have Weisswurst. Do you know what that is?'

'I'm afraid not.'

'White sausage.'

'White?'

Boris laughed. 'Your expression is exactly the same as Miss

Harrison's when I told her about it! We also have Gelbwurst. Yellow sausage.'

'Yellow?'

He laughed again. 'The skin is coloured with saffron. Then we have Regensburger Wurst and Presskopf. And that's just in Bavaria, I could talk some more about the sausages in other parts of Germany. In England you have only... sausage.'

'I think there are some regional types,' said Lottie. 'But I can't think of their names off the top of my head.'

'Gloucester sausage,' said Miss Harrison. 'I think that's one of them.' She pulled a grimace as if she wasn't really sure.

'Please excuse me,' said Boris. 'But I think Prince Manfred needs me. The sooner he learns to speak more languages, the better!' He made his way to where the prince stood with a group of people.

'I hope you don't mind me mentioning this,' Lottie said to Miss Harrison. 'But I found Hector Johnson's jacket the day before he was murdered.'

Miss Harrison frowned. 'Why are you telling me this?'

'Because I found a threatening note in the pocket. And the next day, he was murdered. I'm mentioning it because you were there on the evening he died.'

Miss Harrison sighed. 'I'm never going to escape that fact, am I?'

'I'm sorry for bringing it up.'

'But are you? Or do you have some morbid curiosity about what happened?'

'It's only because I found his jacket, I never met him though. Did you know him well?' Lottie thought about the argument the pair had reportedly had before the poker game.

'Not very well.'

'But a little?'

'Yes. Look, I've been questioned a lot by the police and it's been quite tiring. And I'm under orders to stay here in

Monaco for the time being. I'm stuck here! And all people want to talk about is Hector Johnson. If you must know, there was something between us. And I may as well tell you because you'll probably find out, anyway. He accused me of stealing from him.'

'Really? Stealing what?'

'Money. I'd met him once before and he thought I'd stolen from him. But I hadn't, so I'd like to clear that up now.' Lottie wondered if this had been the reason for the disagreement which Michel Rossi claimed to have witnessed.

The sky had clouded over now and the breeze was growing stronger.

'I don't know who murdered Hector,' continued Miss Harrison. 'But I'm surprised the police haven't caught the culprit yet.'

'Why are you surprised?'

'Someone must have seen something, mustn't they? The murderer must have been agitated afterwards and that can't have gone unnoticed. And someone could have seen the murderer through the window.'

'When?'

'When they were hiding behind the curtain. Anyone sitting at the tables outside the Cafe de Paris could have noticed them.'

'But it was dark.'

'Yes, it was. But in Monte Carlo, there are a lot of lights and people about until the early hours of the morning. I don't understand how something like that could happen in a place which was so busy. And I don't understand why it's taking Commissaire Verrando and his men so long to arrest someone. Perhaps they're incapable of finding the killer.'

The boat slowed and began to turn. 'I think the captain has realised the weather's turning,' said Miss Harrison, looking up at the sky. 'It might even rain.'

'Why did Hector Johnson accuse you of stealing from him?' Lottie asked.

'I don't know! And does it matter? You'll get into trouble going about asking questions. Some people might take offence.'

'I'm sorry if my questions have offended you.'

Miss Harrison fixed her with a sharp gaze. 'It's not me you need to worry about, Miss Sprigg.'

The conversation felt uncomfortable now and Lottie felt relieved by a call to lunch. Salad, seafood and freshly baked bread were laid out on a table covered by a gingham cloth. Everyone ate hurriedly, seemingly aware the clouds above the sea were looming larger and darker.

As soon as lunch was tidied away, the engine went up a gear and the boat lurched on the waves as it navigated its way back to the harbour. The breeze which now blew across the deck was cold and strong.

'Oh dear,' said Mrs Moore, gripping the handrail. 'Do you think we should go inside, Lottie?'

Lottie felt the first few spots of rain on her face. 'Yes.'

Most of the guests had got there before them and were crammed together on long seats which ran the length of the cabin. Boris and another gentleman made way for Mrs Moore and Lottie.

'That's very kind of you,' said Mrs Moore, just getting to the seat in time before the boat lurched to the right. Prince Manfred sat among the guests looking less cheery than usual. He seemed disappointed that the weather was ruining his day trip.

At the front of the cabin, the grey-bearded man gripped the wheel as he determinedly steered them back to the harbour. Some guests attempted to maintain a cheery conversation, but it seemed nobody was enjoying the rising and sinking motion of the boat.

'You wouldn't think it in the Mediterranean, would you?' said Mrs Moore. 'I always assumed it was as calm as a millpond.'

Rosie lay by Lottie's feet, her head on her paws. Her doleful expression suggested she'd sensed the change in mood. Rain now lashed against the cabin windows and Lottie hoped they'd get to the harbour soon. The rise and fall of the boat was making her queasy.

To distract herself, she went over her brief conversation with Grace Harrison. Why had Hector Johnson accused her of stealing money from him? He must have had grounds for suspecting her. What had the circumstances been? Had his accusation been true, and had she murdered him to keep him quiet?

Lottie also didn't like Grace's warning, "It's not me you need to worry about, Miss Sprigg." Who was she referring to? And what did she know which led her to believe this? Lottie gave a shudder.

In her mind, there were several suspects in Hector Johnson's murder. Miss Harrison seemed the most suspicious at the moment, but Madame and Monsieur Rochefort could have had a motive to murder the American. And there was Beatrice to consider, too. Perhaps the driver of the Bentley knew she had done it and had chased after them to wreak his revenge? Beatrice had pretended the chase had been a bit of fun, but had that been bravado?

The case was proving difficult for Lottie because she hadn't met the victim and she didn't know the suspects well either. It was probably a better idea to leave the case to the commissaire. But she couldn't help thinking about the note. It had been written by the murderer and someone had taken it. But who?

The boat journey was growing more uncomfortable. Prince Manfred was almost as white as his sailor suit, and Mrs

Moore had gone quiet. Lottie fixed her eye on the horizon which she could just see out of the cabin window, and did her best to stomach the rocks and lurches of the boat.

By the time they arrived back in the harbour, Mrs Moore was so keen to return to dry land she had no trouble climbing into the launch at all. Eventually, they stood on the jetty in the pouring rain, sheltering under Mrs Moore's parasol.

'Well Lottie, I enjoyed the first half hour. But as for the rest... I think Prince Manfred should check the weather forecast next time.'

Back at the hotel, Mrs Moore went to her room to rest and recover from the rocking of the boat. Lottie went to her room and read her book of detective stories while the bad weather passed overhead. By early evening, the sun was out again and Lottie looked out of her window. She noticed a familiar figure walking along the seafront, it was Henri on his way to work. Lottie grabbed Rosie's lead and hoped she could catch him before he reached the casino.

Chapter Twenty-Five

'OH, HELLO!' Henri grinned when he saw Lottie. 'Are you coming to the casino again soon?'

'I'm not planning to.'

'That's a shame.'

'But I'll walk with you there now.'

'Oh, good.' He looked down at Rosie. 'How's she doing today?'

'She'd have had a better day if she hadn't been stuck out on a boat in the bad weather.'

'You were out in that?'

Lottie told him about Prince Manfred's poorly planned boat trip. 'I managed to speak to Miss Harrison though,' she added. 'She told me that Mr Johnson accused her of stealing money.'

'Really? I wonder why he did that?'

'I don't know. He must have had a reason to but she wouldn't tell me what it was. I'm not sure she'll want to speak to me again, I don't think she liked me asking her questions.'

'I think it's brave of you.'

'Brave or foolish, I haven't decided which yet. Have you heard if the commissaire's made any more progress?'

'Not that I know of. You'd think it would be straightforward, wouldn't you?'

'Sometimes the cases which seem the simplest can be the hardest to work out. And you can have lots of theories, but until you can prove them... they just remain theories.'

They reached the casino, and Lottie gasped when she saw a black Bentley parked outside. She felt sure it was the same car which had chased her and Beatrice down the mountainside.

'Who does that Bentley belong to?' she asked Henri.

'The black one? It's one which Michel has been driving.'

'Michel? It's his car?'

'No, he can't afford a car like that. But one of the customers is letting him drive it for a few days. Michel loves cars, I expect he's taken such an interest in the Bentley that the owner's allowing him to drive it.'

'Is that common for the casino staff to do?'

'Not very common, but it's not unknown. Perhaps Michel did a favour for the owner. And some casino customers can be very generous with their cars and boats, I think it's because they like to show them off.'

Lottie recalled the driver's face. Could it have belonged to Michel Rossi? There was a possibility. But why had he chased her and Beatrice?

'Which reminds me of something I meant to tell you,' continued Henri. 'I found out what happened to that note which was in Hector Johnson's jacket.'

Lottie tore her eyes away from the Bentley. 'Really?'

'Yes. Michel told me he threw it away. He didn't read it and he didn't realise what it was. So there you go, mystery solved.'

But was it? Lottie stared back at the car again. The mystery now seemed more complicated than ever.

Chapter Twenty-Six

MARIE ROCHEFORT WAS tired of waiting for her husband to be arrested. Something had to be done about it, and that was why she was now seated in Commissaire Verrando's office. She had little confidence in his abilities, but he was the most senior police officer in Monaco, so she had to give things a try.

'I feel it's important to explain my plan to you, Commissaire. And it's also extremely important that you don't tell my husband.'

'Very well.' He picked up his pen and notebook, which suggested some interest in what she was about to say. She took this as an encouraging sign.

'The purpose of our visit to Monaco was to meet with Hector Johnson and Philippe Albertini.'

'Your husband arranged to meet Albertini?'

'Yes.'

'And he knew Albertini was a criminal?'

'Yes.'

'So their meeting in the casino the other evening was planned?'

'Yes.'

'Interesting.'

'It is, isn't it? Now let me tell you more. We had met Hector Johnson in Paris a few times. He approached my husband last year because he wanted to sell some of his labour-saving appliances in our department store. It was clear to us that he had a lot of money and that made my husband interested in him.'

'Just your husband?'

'Yes? What are you suggesting?' She glared at him. Surely he couldn't have heard of her affair with Hector?

'I'm not suggesting anything,' said the commissaire. 'I'm merely wishing to understand that it was your husband who was the one who made the business arrangements with him.'

'Yes, I had nothing to do with those discussions. I assist my husband in the running of our department store, but I look after the staff and the day-to-day things. He's responsible for the money and relationships with business partners and all the rest of that.'

'I see.'

'My husband informed me earlier this year that he was interested in investing in a scheme which Philippe Albertini was setting up.'

'What sort of scheme?'

'I don't know. But knowing Albertini, it's some sort of racketeering scheme. Nothing legal, put it that way. And do you know what, Commissaire? When my husband told me about this latest plan, I decided I'd had enough. For years, I turned a blind eye while he associated himself with all manner of unpleasant, dangerous people just to make more money. And not only does he involve himself in these deeds, but he also drags in other people who have been busy earning an honest living. Hector Johnson, for example.'

Were his eyelids growing heavier, or was she imagining it? Perhaps it was the effect of his thick-lensed glasses.

She continued, 'Hector had built his wealth and success on honest hard work and then my husband decided he should persuade him to put his money into Albertini's scheme. I'd seen enough! And that's when I contacted the Parisian police and told them everything. I explained to them we had this visit to Monaco planned, and they passed that information to the police in Marseille. The Marseille police have been watching Albertini for many years, it seems they'd rather do that than arrest him for anything. Anyway, it was agreed that, in return for my cooperation, I would escape prosecution for any of the charges levelled against my husband after his arrest. Not that I am guilty of much. At the very worst, I didn't inform the police about my husband's criminal investments. My conscience has got the better of me these days and I am cooperating fully with every police officer I come across. It is time that justice is done!'

She opened her cigarette case and pulled out a cigarette. It was at this point when she noticed the commissaire's eyes were practically closed.

'Commissaire?'

He jolted. 'Yes?'

'Did you listen to every single word I said?'

'Yes.'

'Then why didn't you write any of it down in your little notebook?'

'I was waiting for you to finish.'

'You can remember everything I've just told you?'

'Yes.'

'Good. So that means I am completely exonerated and won't face any charges for anything whatsoever?'

'Well, that depends.'

'On what?'

'On whether you had something to do with Hector Johnson's murder.'

'Of course I didn't! What nonsense.'

'What about your husband?'

'My husband?' She inhaled on her cigarette. 'I feel terrible saying this, Commissaire. But I'm really not sure about him at all.'

'You think he could have murdered Mr Johnson?'

'I have no evidence that he did it. But do I believe he could have done it?' She sighed for effect and then gave a sniff before continuing, 'Sadly, I think he could have done.'

'Why would he murder him?'

'There are two reasons.'

'Two?' The commissaire seemed a little more awake now.

'The first reason is because Hector could have told the police about my husband's criminal dealings. Once Hector realised Albertini was a criminal, he refused to invest his money into his scheme. There was also a danger he could report my husband to the authorities. That worried my husband greatly.'

'And the second reason?'

'Hector and I were having a love affair. My husband was terribly jealous of it. So you see, he had a powerful motive for wanting Hector dead.' She gave a sob and pulled out a handkerchief to cover her dry eyes. 'I can't believe I'm having to admit this to you, Commissaire. I feel such a traitor!'

Chapter Twenty-Seven

'THAT RAINFALL this afternoon was fun, wasn't it?' said Beatrice at dinner that evening. 'My tyres couldn't grip the road at all and the Bugatti was sliding around all over the place! I expect you're relieved you weren't with me today, Lottie!'

'Yes. Although I've discovered the identity of the driver who was chasing us yesterday.'

'Chasing us? He was just having a bit of fun.'

'It didn't sound like fun to me,' said Mrs Moore.

'That's because you're not a motorist. Believe me, when you're a motorist, such things don't bother you at all. Who was he anyway?'

'Michel Rossi,' said Lottie. 'He was the dealer at your poker game with Mr Johnson.'

'Oh, him!' Her brow furrowed. 'What was he doing racing around in a Bentley?'

'Apparently, one of the casino customers has lent it to him.'

'Have they? I wonder who they are. I wouldn't mind a

spin in it myself. It's clearly a perk of the job that he gets to race around in vehicles like that.'

'But why do you think he chased us? I've met Michel, and he seems a pleasant, well-mannered man.'

'People can change as soon as they get behind the wheel. It can sometimes bring out a competitive nature.'

'That still doesn't explain why he drove like he did. He wanted us to stop, didn't he?'

'He seemed to. Or maybe he was just playing about. I'm surprised to have discovered that it was the poker dealer of all people. But there you go. I'm just pleased he didn't do it today with all the rain on the road. There's no doubt we'd have tumbled down the mountainside.'

'Do you think the reason he chased us could have had something to do with Hector Johnson's death?' Lottie asked.

'No. Why?'

'Maybe Michel thinks you murdered Mr Johnson and wanted to have his revenge?'

'Why would he think that?'

'I don't know. It's just an idea.'

'A silly idea, if you ask me.'

'But let's pretend for a moment that it could be true,' said Mrs Moore.

'But if we do pretend that I murdered Hector Johnson, why would Michel seek revenge for that?'

'Perhaps the pair were good friends?' suggested Mrs Moore.

'You'd have to ask Michel about that. I've no idea if the pair were good friends or not.'

'Beatrice,' said Mrs Moore. 'Don't you ever wonder who murdered Hector Johnson?'

'Yes, all the time! I know it wasn't me, so I suppose it could have been the Rocheforts or that young Harrison girl.'

'Or Michel?' said Mrs Moore.

'Yes, it could have been him, I suppose,' said Beatrice.

'Maybe Michel murdered Mr Johnson and is worried you saw him do something suspicious, so he wants to murder you too?'

Beatrice frowned. 'But I thought the two were friends?'

'They might have been.'

'You're now suggesting Michel murdered Mr Johnson?'

'Yes.'

'Why would he do that?'

'I don't know,' said Mrs Moore. 'But maybe Michel tried to murder you yesterday to stop you from giving any evidence against him.'

'What evidence?'

'I don't know.'

Beatrice took a swig from her drink. 'The pair of you are confusing me now. One minute Michel wants to murder me for revenge for something I didn't do and the next he wants to murder me to stop me providing evidence even though I don't have any.'

'They're just theories,' said Mrs Moore with a sigh.

'Well, if that's all they are, then why waste time thinking about them? Leave it to the police, that's what I say. We came to Monaco for a good time, didn't we?'

'Yes,' said Mrs Moore. 'I suppose we did.'

'Then let's have a good time!' Beatrice raised her glass. 'Cheers! As they say in Britain. Do they say that in America, too?'

'Yes, they do,' said Mrs Moore, picking up her drink. 'Cheers.'

'Oh look who it is!' said Beatrice, her attention now on the restaurant door. 'Madame and Monsieur Rochefort!' Lottie turned to see the stylish French couple speaking to a waiter.

'They can come and join us here,' said Beatrice, getting up and marching over to them.

Lottie's heart sank. She hadn't seen the couple since she'd had the uncomfortable discussion with them in the lobby of their hotel.

'They're the French couple who played poker with Beatrice and Hector Johnson on the night he died?' Mrs Moore asked Lottie.

'Yes.'

'Goodness. So they could be murder suspects too?'

'They could be.'

'Golly. I'm not sure how I feel about dining with three murder suspects. It makes me a little uneasy.'

Lottie realised she hadn't told Mrs Moore that she'd visited the Rocheforts at their hotel. She hoped they wouldn't mention it.

She watched as Beatrice led them over, accompanied by a waiter. Beatrice carried out the introductions while the waiter joined two tables together for them to sit at.

Marie Rochefort was dressed in mauve and looked beautiful, yet aloof. Sour-faced Joseph Rochefort wore a smart black suit.

'So what are you doing at the Hôtel de Paris?' Beatrice asked them. 'Is the restaurant at your hotel not as good as this one?'

'It's perfectly good,' said Monsieur Rochefort. 'We're at the Metropole. But we've heard excellent things about this restaurant, so we thought we'd come and try it. Ideally, we'd be back in Paris by now, but the commissaire is insisting we stay here until he catches the murderer. How long is that going to take?'

'It feels like forever!' said Beatrice. 'Your shop must be missing you.'

'You have a shop?' Mrs Moore asked them.

'Yes,' said Madame Rochefort. 'It's a department store, actually. The largest in Paris.'

'Really? Good golly. Lottie and I were in Paris only recently, weren't we Lottie? We should have dropped in, although we didn't have a lot of time there.'

'Perhaps next time you visit?'

'Oh yes, we'll be there. Without a doubt! What's it called?'

'Rochefort.'

'Ah, that's easy then! I shan't forget. It's so much easier to name a business after oneself, isn't it?'

'My grandfather founded the store,' said Monsieur Rochefort. 'And I inherited it.'

'What a thing to inherit! If only my father had owned an enormous store rather than built railroads.'

'Railroads?'

'Yes, he was a railroad tycoon. And thankfully, I didn't inherit any railroads. If I had, I wouldn't have known what to do with them!'

'You just inherited the money instead?'

'Yes. I was grateful for that.'

'And Miss Sprigg is your daughter?'

'Oh no. She's my travelling companion.'

'Ah.'

Lottie squirmed a little under Monsieur Rochefort's scrutinising gaze.

The waiter took their order and everyone listened as Beatrice recounted a tale of her precarious drive in the rainy mountains.

'It's good news you didn't come to any harm,' said Madame Rochefort.

'Talking of coming to harm,' said Mrs Moore. 'I hear you were playing poker with Hector Johnson on the night he died.'

'That's right.'

'Have you any idea who murdered him?'

Monsieur Rochefort spread his palms. 'Does anyone?'

'It seems not,' added his wife. 'Not even the commissaire.'

'Which is most odd,' said Mrs Moore. 'When you consider there were only a few of you in the room.'

'Well, it wasn't me, if that's what you're suggesting,' said Madame Rochefort.

'Oh no, I wasn't suggesting such a thing!'

'Or my husband.'

'Of course not.'

'Or me,' piped up Beatrice. 'If you ask me, then I think it was a lunatic who crept in there during the day and hid behind the curtain until he got his opportunity.'

'You think a lunatic was behind the curtain for the entire time we were playing poker?' asked Madame Rochefort with a shudder.

'He could have been.'

'What a dreadful thought! I think the casino staff should be checking behind curtains.'

'They probably are now.'

'I don't understand how a so-called lunatic would creep into the casino and hide for all that time,' said Monsieur Rochefort. 'And why would he murder Mr Johnson?'

'I've no idea,' said Beatrice. 'It's merely a thought. Earlier, I was listening to some theories these two ladies came up with.' She gestured at Lottie and Mrs Moore. 'And they had me completely confused.'

'You were suggesting theories, were you, Mrs Moore?' said Monsieur Rochefort. Then he gave Lottie a sharp glance.

'I'm afraid so,' said Mrs Moore. 'The tragic event must have become the talk of the town now. Especially because they haven't caught the person who did it. And don't underestimate young Lottie here, she actually has quite a talent for working these things out.'

'Is that right?'

Lottie felt an urge to shrink down beneath the table, away from Monsieur Rochefort's gaze.

Chapter Twenty-Eight

THE BRIGHT MORNING sunshine helped clear Lottie's head as she walked along the seafront with Rosie. She hadn't slept well. She'd been trying to fathom why Michel Rossi had chased her and Beatrice along the mountain roads. Had he been after her or Beatrice? Or had it merely been a bit of fun, as Beatrice had suggested?

It hadn't felt like fun. And whose car had he been driving? Lottie wondered if she was feeling brave enough to ask him. She also wanted to know why he'd thrown away the note which had been in Hector Johnson's jacket pocket.

The more she thought about Michel, the more she realised he could be the murderer.

He'd admitted he'd been the last person to leave the poker room. Perhaps he hadn't left it at all? Maybe he'd waited in there for Hector Johnson to return. And was Michel really to be believed when he said he hadn't noticed Mr Johnson's reading glasses had been left there? How could he have failed to notice them? If he was innocent, then he would have picked them up and given them to Mr Johnson. If he was guilty, however, then it made sense that he would have wanted them to stay where they were, so Mr Johnson would have to return to the room.

But if Michel had murdered Mr Johnson, what had his motive been? Had Hector Johnson caused him some personal inconvenience? Or had Michel carried out the murder on the orders of someone else?

Lottie thought about the casino owner, Mr Blanchard. She'd met him once, and he hadn't seemed very friendly. Was it possible he'd ordered Michel to murder Mr Johnson? Being unfriendly didn't mean he was a murderer, but he was someone to consider.

They passed the repaired section of wall and Lottie noticed Grace Harrison walking towards her from the direction of the harbour. Lottie suspected Miss Harrison wouldn't have much to say to her after their conversation on the boat had turned uncomfortable. But Miss Harrison stopped and patted Rosie.

They exchanged a few words about the pleasant nature of the morning, then Miss Harrison said, 'I'm pleased I've bumped into you this morning. I wish to apologise for my rudeness yesterday.'

'I don't recall you being rude,' said Lottie. 'I asked you some searching questions and I can understand why you didn't want to be quizzed by me.'

'I feel I was rude. It's not what I'm usually like. In fact, I haven't felt quite myself since the events of the other evening.'

'That's understandable.'

'I feel like I have too much to think about at the moment. Do you mind if I walk with you for a little while?'

'Not at all. How about we walk to the terraces behind the casino?'

'That would be nice.'

They went on their way. Across the road, Lottie spotted Commissaire Verrando speaking to a policeman. He glanced briefly in their direction but Miss Harrison didn't notice him. 'I hope you don't mind, but I need to talk about something,' continued the young woman. 'I barely know you, Lottie, but you seem friendly, and I've been awfully lonely. The truth is... I'm not a nice person.'

This wasn't something Lottie had been expecting to hear. 'Why not?'

'I'm not who I say I am.'

'Who are you?'

'I'm Grace Harrison, I haven't lied about that. But I'm a criminal.'

'Oh.'

'When Hector Johnson accused me of stealing from him, he was right.'

'He was?'

'We went to dinner together a few days before he died. He left his jacket on his chair while he went to the bathroom and I'm afraid to say I stole some money from his wallet, which he left in his pocket.'

'I see. Why are you telling me this?'

'Because I feel so bad about it! I feel like I have to tell someone. I denied it when he confronted me and that makes me feel even worse because then he died. I feel so guilty! And there's nothing I can do now to make amends.'

'You could tell the police.'

'They'd arrest me and fine me. I don't have the money for a fine. Stealing is how I make my living. I'm a thief and it's what I was doing in London before I decided to try my luck in Paris.'

'You must make a lot of money from it,' said Lottie. 'How else would the casino have allowed you to play high stakes poker in one of its private rooms?'

'Yes, I have made a lot. And it's all stolen. To be honest

with you, I'm a good thief. And I enjoy nice clothes, restaurants and hotels.'

'How did you get into this state?'

'Life was hard when I was a child. I was abandoned as a baby and I grew up in an orphanage. I felt unwanted. And what I craved more than anything were nice things. I didn't have a proper education, only the few lessons they taught us in the schoolroom in the orphanage. Some of the older girls there used to take me to the streets in London's West End and we would steal things from the department stores. Things like silk handkerchiefs and small china ornaments. They were easy to fit into our pockets and easy to sell too. When I saw the rich ladies who shopped in the department stores, I wanted to be just like them. But I didn't see how I could achieve it without stealing.'

'I think you've very brave for telling me this.'

'I'm not brave. I'm a coward! I'm only telling you because... I don't know, I feel like I'll explode if I don't tell someone soon. But I'm determined to mend my ways now. The fact that Mr Johnson was murdered has changed everything for me. I won't ever get over my guilt about the way I treated him.'

'We're not too dissimilar, you know.'

'We're not?'

'I grew up in an orphanage too.'

'You did?' She raised her eyebrows. 'I never would have guessed!'

'It's difficult to guess someone's an orphan, isn't it?'

'Yes it is. But look at the difference between us. We're both in Monaco, but I've lied and stolen to get here while you're here because you've worked hard.'

'Travelling with Mrs Moore doesn't feel like hard work.'

'But you've worked at it and you're a good person. You must be happy you've found something you enjoy.'

Lottie smiled. 'I am.'

They paused and looked out over the sea. Lottie felt quite taken aback that this woman she barely knew had confided so much. Perhaps it was because she was lonely. And maybe she felt drawn to another young woman from England.

But was Miss Harrison being honest? She seemed genuine, but Lottie had to remember she'd made good money from her dishonesty.

'You mentioned you met Prince Manfred at the casino,' Lottie said. 'You weren't planning to steal from him as well, were you?'

Miss Harrison lowered her head. 'I'm afraid I was. That's why I befriended him. But I discovered he has quite a few people with him and his interpreter is always there. I decided not to do it. But he clearly considered that he was friendly enough with me to invite me on his boat trip yesterday. I've resolved now that I won't do it anymore. I'm going to turn over a new leaf. I'm going to stop lying and stealing. Mr Johnson's death has decided it for me. It's going to be difficult to no longer have nice things, but I shall grow accustomed to it. I've just moved to a room at the cheapest hotel I could find here, the Hôtel Riviera. And when I leave Monaco, I'll find a proper, honest job which won't pay much, but I'll be able to live my life free of guilt.'

'That sounds like a sensible idea, Miss Harrison,' said Lottie.

'Call me Grace.'

'Alright then.'

They exchanged a smile, then turned back to the sea.

'Do you think Hector Johnson had any idea that someone wished to murder him?' Lottie asked Grace.

'I don't think so. Although he told me about something strange which happened.'

'What was that?'

'Apparently, he was walking up from the harbour when a car came off the road and almost hit him. He only just managed to jump out of the way in time.'

'Goodness.'

'And he told me he didn't think it was an accident. He thought someone had driven at him on purpose!'

Chapter Twenty-Nine

'WHAT'S GOING ON HERE?'

Beatrice heard the voice as she lay on the ground beneath her car. She turned her head and saw a pair of shiny gentleman's shoes.

'Who is it?' she called out.

'You're a lady?'

'Yes, I'm a lady! What of it?'

'Well it's even more of a disgrace then.'

The oil had just finished draining into the tray next to her head. She fixed the oil drain plug into place, then wriggled out from beneath her vehicle.

The gentleman looked down his nose at her. 'Don't I recognise you?' he said.

'Yes you do, Mr Blanchard.' She got to her feet, wrench in hand. 'I'm one of your best customers. Beatrice de Cambry de Baudimont.'

'But you're wearing overalls!'

'Because I'm carrying out an oil change on my car.'

'Here? Right outside the Hôtel de Paris? In the Place du Casino in the very centre of Monte Carlo? This is one of the most exclusive places in Europe and you're treating it like a mechanic's shed!'

'Where else am I supposed to change the oil?'

'Get a man to do it in a garage somewhere.'

'I don't need a man to do it, I'm quite capable of doing it myself. And besides, I won't let anybody else touch this Bugatti. I know the placement and condition of every wire, nut and bolt.'

'Well, perhaps you can have a word with the hotel manager and see if he can find you a shed or somewhere similar where you can work on it. The sight of someone lying prostrate in oil-covered overalls beneath their car brings down the tone of the area. I don't know what my customers will think when they arrive at the casino later.'

'I'll have washed and scrubbed myself by then, Mr Blanchard.'

'And wiped the oil off your face, I hope.'

'No, I like to leave it there, it's good for the complexion.' She put her hands on her hips and glared at him, waiting to rebuff the next attack.

'Well, perhaps I shall have a word with the manager about the provision of a facility where his guests can work on their cars out of view.'

'Yes, you do that, Mr Blanchard. And, in the meantime, maybe you can have a word with your employee Michel Rossi?'

'What's he done?'

'Chased me in a Bentley 3 Litre Tourer, that's what.'

'Where did he get that from?'

'Apparently one of your customers has lent it to him.'

'I see. What colour is it?'

'Black.'

'In which case, I think I've seen it parked outside the

casino, but I didn't realise he was driving it. He was chasing you?'

'Yes. Two days ago. I realise it was probably only a game, but he frightened my young passenger.'

'I'll have a word with him.'

'As well as the hotel manager?'

'Yes.'

'I'm looking forward to seeing which shed he's able to provide me with.'

Mr Blanchard went on his way and Beatrice clambered back beneath her car and gave the oil drain plug an extra turn with her wrench to make sure it was securely on.

Why had Michel Rossi chased her down the mountain road? She'd pretended to the English girl that it had been a bit of fun, but that was only because she hadn't wanted to show she was frightened. He'd been driving so recklessly, they could have been killed. Fortunately, her driving skills had got them out of it. What a foolish man he was! She hoped that a word from Mr Blanchard would prevent him from doing such a thing again.

But would that be enough? Michel Rossi was clearly a dangerous man.

Chapter Thirty

'I'D LIKE to visit the casino again this evening,' Lottie said to Mrs Moore at lunchtime.

'Why?'

'Because I want to ask the casino dealer, Michel, why he chased me and Beatrice in his car.'

'You want to confront him?'

'No, I don't like confrontations. I would like to ask him politely and see what he says.'

'He tried to drive you off the road, Lottie. I think you need to stay out of his way.'

'But I'd like to hear an explanation from him! He can't cause me much harm if we're in the casino.'

'He could do. Look what happened to Hector Johnson! I think it's best to tell the police and then forget about it.'

'But what if he had something to do with Hector Johnson's death?'

'Let the police deal with it.'

'But I found that note in Mr Johnson's jacket which threatened him with murder and I've discovered now that

Michel removed the note from the jacket! I'd like to ask him about that too.'

Mrs Moore gave a sigh. 'I can tell you're quite determined about this, Lottie.'

'Yes, I am.'

'And if you hadn't had such successes in Venice, Paris and Cairo, then I would refuse.'

'But?' Lottie grew hopeful.

'But seeing as this is something you're determined to do, then I shall allow it. And I shall accompany you too, I don't want you speaking to a dangerous man alone.'

'Thank you.'

Mrs Moore tucked into her salade niçoise. 'The casino would be much more fun with Prince Manfred. But I haven't heard from him since yesterday's disastrous boat trip. I'm worried he's still upset about it.'

LOTTIE WAS EXCITED to wear her sequinned gown again. Mrs Moore chose a raspberry red dress for the occasion, the bodice was decorated with countless little silk roses.

'Oh, how I'm tempted to play roulette again!' she said as they stepped into the opulent entrance hall of the casino. Rosie trotted by their side. 'I suppose we could watch people play, couldn't we? It's not quite the same as having a go yourself, though. And to think I was so critical of Prince Manfred's gambling! I've learned now it can be wonderful fun.'

'As long as you're gambling with someone else's money.'

'Absolutely, Lottie. It must always be someone else's money, otherwise you're on the road to ruin.'

As they made their way to the roulette tables, Lottie was pleased to spot Henri.

'You're looking extremely... wonderful again this evening, Lottie,' he said. She felt bashful.

'I'd like to speak to Michel, is he here this evening?'

'I think he's on the baccarat table. I'll ask him when his next break is. You should try your hand at a game while you wait.'

'No thank you, I'd be hopeless.'

'You might not be.'

'I don't want to risk finding out!'

Henri returned while Lottie was watching a game of roulette with Mrs Moore.

'Michel has a break in about ten minutes.'

'Thank you, Henri.'

'I can't talk any longer, there are a lot of ashtrays which need emptying.'

'That's fine.' She smiled. 'I won't keep you from your work.'

'He seems a polite young man,' said Mrs Moore. 'And I think he has eyes for you too, Lottie.'

'I'm sure he doesn't.'

'Oh goodness! It isn't, is it?' Mrs Moore picked up her lorgnette. 'Yes it is! Prince Manfred is here!'

The prince strode in with his entourage, looking much happier than he had the previous day on his boat. Instead of his damp sailor suit, he now wore a shiny, topaz blue satin jacket with white trousers, shirt and waistcoat.

'Mrs Moore!' He kissed her hand and Boris, the interpreter, explained they had just called in at the hotel to ask if she would like to accompany the prince this evening.

'You should have given me some notice and then I would have been there waiting for you!' she replied. Then, to her obvious delight, they made their way to the roulette table.

Lottie watched Mrs Moore move the prince's chips around the table before realising the time and going off to find Michel. She soon spotted him, but Beatrice was talking to him. As she watched, Lottie was reminded of how mild-mannered he seemed. Could he really have been the man who'd chased them on the mountain roads?

Beatrice caught sight of Lottie and smiled. 'Ah, hello, Lottie. I was just congratulating Mr Rossi here on his driving skills. You recall that rather risky adventure the other day, don't you?'

Lottie nodded.

'Well, Mr Rossi says he mistook us for someone else.'

'Who?'

Beatrice turned back to him. 'Miss Sprigg has a point. Who did you think we were?'

'A customer at the casino who we had trouble with.'

'You're telling me they also drove a red Bugatti?'

'It was a small red motor car, I don't know the type.'

Beatrice gave Lottie a sidelong glance which suggested she didn't believe him. Then she turned back to Michel. 'Even if you did think I was a customer you'd had trouble with, don't you think it was rather dangerous to carry on in that way? You could have caused a serious accident.'

'I suppose my emotions got the better of me. It was a customer who we thought had been cheating the casino and that sort of thing makes me very angry.'

'Strange. You don't strike me as the angry type, Michel.'

'Well, I can be when I'm provoked.'

'Did you do it because you thought I murdered Hector Johnson?'

'What? No! I don't think you murdered him at all. And besides, I didn't even know it was you in the car. I apologise for that, it was a case of mistaken identity.' He checked his watch. 'I need to get back to my table.'

'Just one quick thing,' said Lottie.

'Yes?' His blue eyes looked weary.

'I believe you took something from Hector Johnson's jacket,' said Lottie.

'His jacket? What would I want with his jacket?'

'I found it under a bench the day before he died,' said Lottie. 'I handed it to the doorman and it was returned to the cloakroom. Apparently, at some point, you took the note out of it and threw it away.'

'I remember now. Yes I did, that's correct. I didn't realise the note was important.'

'Didn't you check before you decided to throw it away?'

'I did check, but it was written in English, I think, and I didn't understand it. I thought it was nothing. What did it say?'

'The note was from someone threatening Hector Johnson.'

'Really?' He blew out a sigh. 'That is a surprise indeed. I'm afraid I didn't know, I'm sorry.' He checked his watch again. 'I really must get back to work.'

Lottie watched him leave.

'I don't know about you, Lottie,' said Beatrice. 'But I think that man has just told us a heap of lies.'

Chapter Thirty-One

FOR A FEW MOMENTS, Grace Harrison wondered where she was when she woke. The hotel room was much smaller and simpler than she was used to. Then she remembered she'd moved to the cheapest room in Monaco's cheapest hotel. It wasn't particularly cheap when compared with hotels elsewhere, but she was doing what she could to save money.

Today was the first day of her new life. An honest life in which she lived modestly. And when she could finally leave Monaco, she would return to London and find a normal job.

Hector Johnson's death had changed her. She couldn't live with the guilt of her former lifestyle. So from now on, she had to make amends. Perhaps she could help people rather than take from them.

She pulled open the curtains. She no longer had a view of the sea, which was a shame. Instead, she looked out over a mediocre street with very little going on. She couldn't even see an expensive boutique or a fancy restaurant. She had somehow found the most ordinary corner of Monaco possible.

Grace had begun sorting through her belongings the previous evening and they were still strewn across the floor.

She pulled back the bedcovers and sat up, surveying the mess. She'd made a pile of papers which could link her to her crimes. They had to be destroyed before anyone could find them. She got down onto the floor and began ripping them up into tiny pieces and dropping them into the wastepaper basket. Even her diary had to be destroyed.

Then her heart gave a heavy thud when she came across the note:

I warned you but you didn't listen, now you're for it.

Her mouth felt dry as she read it again. She recalled the horrible cold lurch in her stomach when she'd first read it. Should the note be destroyed? Perhaps she should keep it. Just in case.

As Grace continued ripping up the other papers, she wondered if she'd told Lottie too much. She'd taken a risk in confiding in her, but she'd been holding too many secrets to keep them to herself. She'd felt a lot better since she'd spoken to Lottie, as if she had lifted a burden. Although she felt guilty about Hector Johnson, she felt a little better now that she'd confessed to Lottie that she'd stolen his money.

She had to hope Lottie wouldn't tell anyone else. She'd chosen her because she was friendly and easy to talk to. She had to hope Lottie would keep it to herself and not tell the police. And even if she did, surely Grace could just deny it? It would become one person's word against another's.

Chapter Thirty-Two

'DID I see you spending more of Prince Manfred's money in the casino last night?' Beatrice asked Mrs Moore at lunch.

'I'm afraid so!' she chuckled. 'I didn't add it up, but it was quite a large amount.'

'And the prince didn't mind?'

'No, he didn't mind at all! In fact, he told me that I help him!'

'Is that so?'

'Yes, he says I have a skill for roulette. And I must say that, having had no idea what the game was a week ago, I now have quite an intricate understanding of it. I know how to place the best bets.'

'But it's just a ball rolling around a wheel,' said Lottie. 'Surely it's down to luck?'

'Yes, but some people are extra lucky,' said Beatrice. 'And that certainly appears to be the case with Roberta. Now I wonder if we can get some more sandwiches? My drive this morning has worked up quite an appetite.'

'Even though you were sitting down?' said Mrs Moore.

'Yes, it's extremely tiring.'

'How?'

'The concentration. Taking a hairpin bend at forty miles an hour takes a lot of focus.'

'That's a ridiculous speed to be driving around a bend at.'

'Perhaps I'm exaggerating a little.'

'I don't think you are, Beatrice,' said Lottie. 'I've been in the car with you.'

Beatrice laughed and summoned the waiter. 'It's a relief to see you here, Madame de Cambry de Baudimont,' he said.

'Really? Why?'

'Because there's been an accident on the road. I worried you might have been involved, but thankfully not.'

'That's nice of you to say so, but awfully sad about the accident,' said Beatrice. 'When did it happen?'

'About midday. Apparently, the car came off a mountain road and rolled downhill.'

'Oh no! Were the people in the car alright?'

'I don't know, I'm afraid. But if your car comes off a mountain road, then usually...' He pulled a grimace. 'Usually it's not a good outcome.'

Lottie recalled the steepness of the roads and the sheer drops she had seen as they turned each bend. She gave a shudder.

Another waiter approached their table.

'Golly, we're popular today, aren't we?' said Mrs Moore.

The second waiter addressed Lottie. 'You have a visitor, Miss Sprigg. I'm sorry to disturb you, but he says it's quite urgent.'

As Lottie made her way to the lobby, she wondered who her visitor could be. The commissaire perhaps? Or Monsieur Rochefort? The thought of seeing him gave her a shiver.

She was relieved to see Henri waiting for her in the lobby, but he looked serious.

'Is everything alright?' she asked.

'Not really. Have you heard about the accident?'

'Yes. What happened?'

'It was Michel.'

Lottie startled. 'Michel Rossi?'

'He went out for a drive and lost control on a bend. There was no one else involved.'

'Is he...'

'Dead? Yes, he is.'

'How awful! I'm so sorry to hear it. You must be very shocked.'

'Everyone at the casino is shocked. He wasn't my best friend, but I'm upset about it. I don't know how the accident happened. Michel was used to driving on those roads, I know he didn't always drive sensibly but he was very familiar with them.'

'IT'S A COMPLETE WRECK?' said Joseph Rochefort to the police officer. 'What did he do to it?'

'He came off the road, and the car fell about a hundred feet.'

'How did he come off the road?'

'We think he lost control on a bend.'

'But he was a good driver!'

'That may be so, but sometimes something can happen. A distraction perhaps... or even something wrong with the car.'

'There was nothing wrong with my car!'

'Perhaps it had a mechanical fault which you weren't aware of, Monsieur Rochefort?'

'I paid a lot of money for that car. It shouldn't have had a fault. Now what are my wife and I going to drive back to Paris in?'

'I'm afraid I can't help with that. Was there some form of insurance cover for the car?'

'I don't think so. I didn't think anything would go wrong with it. And I certainly didn't expect someone to drive it down a cliff!'

'It was an accident, monsieur.'

Joseph sighed. He'd entrusted Michel with the care of that car, and now it was an unsalvageable wreck. Everything had gone wrong for him since he'd arrived in Monaco.

LOTTIE REFLECTED on the accident as she took Rosie out for a stroll after lunch. Over the past few days, she'd been growing more convinced that Michel had murdered Hector Johnson. Was it possible he'd driven the car off the bend to escape justice?

She shivered at the thought. If it was so, then the mystery of Mr Johnson's murder was unlikely to ever be solved.

Had someone else caused Michel's accident? It was possible that another car had been involved and then sped off before the wreckage was found.

She couldn't ignore the fact that Beatrice had been out for a drive that morning. Could she have chased after Michel in revenge for his driving a few days ago? She didn't like to think Beatrice was capable of such a thing, but she knew it had to be considered.

Beatrice had seemed her normal, chatty self at lunchtime. Could she really have forced Michel's car off the road and then returned to the hotel and carried on as if nothing had happened? That could only be the action of an extremely cold-hearted, callous person.

Lottie reached the part of the wall which had been repaired after a car had hit it. Then she recalled a waiter at the hotel mentioning that it had been a lot quieter in Monaco while Beatrice's car was being repaired. Had Beatrice hit the wall? She also recalled Grace Harrison telling her that Hector Johnson had escaped being hit by a car. She wondered if there could be a connection.

The boutique clothes shop where Mrs Moore had bought Lottie's dress was opposite. 'Come along Rosie,' she said. 'Let's see what they can tell us about the accident.'

'I WAS HERE WHEN IT HAPPENED,' said the shop assistant with dark eyeliner. 'A red car hit the wall. I think it was that noisy red car which has been zooming around the place for the past fortnight.'

'I heard the car nearly hit someone,' said the other assistant.

'How awful. Do you know who he was?'

'I think he was an American tourist.'

Lottie felt a pang of excitement as she began to piece together the information. Unless she was mistaken, a car matching the description of Beatrice's car had almost hit a man similar to Hector Johnson. She knew Beatrice's car had been repaired recently, and she knew Mr Johnson had escaped a similar accident. Could it have been an attempt by Beatrice to murder the American businessman? And, having failed, was it Beatrice who had then murdered him in the casino? And had she now murdered Michel Rossi? It was beginning to look that way, but Lottie couldn't understand the reason why.

'Is there anything else we can help with?' asked the first assistant. 'We have some new handbags on display if you'd like to look at them?'

'No thank you, another time,' said Lottie, aware that she was now lost in her thoughts. 'Thank you for your help.'

Chapter Thirty-Three

With theories racing through her mind, Lottie was glad to bump into Henri again after leaving the dress shop. She told him her thoughts about Beatrice being the murderer.

'The racing car woman did it?' he asked. 'But why?'

'I don't know.'

'You have to find out why.'

'I realise that, but I don't know how to go about it.'

'You could try asking her.'

'If she's responsible for two murders? I don't think she'll take kindly to that.'

'Just ask her about the time she drove her car into the wall and see what she says. And there's no evidence that Michel was murdered. Everyone is assuming it was an accident.'

'But an unusual accident for someone who knew the roads so well, don't you think? I saw him drive and I could tell he was skilled at it. Do you know who the Bentley belonged to?'

'Yes, I found out earlier. And you'll be surprised.'

'Will I?'

'The car belonged to Madame and Monsieur Rochefort.'

'Really?'

'Apparently Monsieur Rochefort is upset about the loss of his car.'

'And not upset about the loss of Michel Rossi?'

'Maybe he is, I don't know.'

'Did Michel ever mention the Rocheforts to you?'

'No, never.'

'Why did Monsieur Rochefort lend Michel his car?'

'I don't know. Perhaps Rochefort foolishly assumed that being friendly with a casino croupier might bring him rewards? It doesn't work like that, though. Maybe Michel did a favour for him?'

'Such as what?'

'I wish I knew. It feels frustrating to know only half the story.'

'I know exactly what you mean.'

'And perhaps it's irrelevant, anyway. If you're so sure the Belgian motor lady is the murderer, then perhaps the case is solved.'

'Perhaps.'

BACK AT THE HOTEL, Lottie found Mrs Moore having a drink with Beatrice in the lounge. It was apparent the two ladies were getting on well and Lottie felt wary about asking Beatrice uncomfortable questions. She didn't want to ruin things, but felt she had little choice. If Beatrice was a murderer, then Lottie felt duty bound to help reveal it.

'Do come and join us, Lottie,' said Mrs Moore. 'Beatrice was just explaining to me how to play. Oh, what's the name of it again?'

'Vingt-un,' said Beatrice. 'Or Twenty-One.'

'It sounds like another casino game I'd be lucky at with Prince Manfred's money,' said Mrs Moore.

'Don't you think it's about time you used your own money?' asked Beatrice.

'No, absolutely not. If I use my money, then that might be bad luck. Whereas using Prince Manfred's money always brings me luck.'

'I think you're turning into a proper gambler now, Roberta.'

'What makes you say that?'

'Because you have superstitions! The true mark of a gambler is when you develop superstitions. Never sit with your legs crossed while gambling and never whistle, either.'

'I can't whistle.'

'Good, there's no chance of it bringing you bad luck then.'

'Whistling while gambling is bad luck?'

'It certainly is.'

'And it's annoying too.'

'It can be. It depends on how accomplished the whistler is. Waiter!' Beatrice ordered some more drinks and Lottie took advantage of the break in the conversation.

'I went into the dress shop earlier,' she said.

'You'd like another outfit?' said Mrs Moore.

'No, I was just browsing. And I happened to speak to the shop assistants about an incident which happened opposite the shop.'

'What was that?'

'A car hit the wall.'

'Oh yes, that was me!' said Beatrice with a laugh.

Lottie hadn't expected her to so readily admit to it.

'Was your car badly damaged?' asked Mrs Moore.

'Not too badly. I wasn't looking where I was going. Terrible isn't it? Fortunately, the outcome wasn't as devastating as it was for Michel Rossi, but it just goes to show how easily these accidents can happen.'

'I heard an odd coincidence, though,' said Lottie. 'Apparently, Hector Johnson only just jumped out of the way at the last minute.'

'Is that so?' Mrs Moore raised her eyebrows.

'An exaggeration,' said Beatrice. 'He was on the path at the time, but it wasn't as close as that.'

'Hector Johnson was walking on the path and you almost hit him?' said Mrs Moore.

'I was quite a distance from him.'

'How far?'

'About three feet.'

'*Three feet*? I don't call that much distance. And how fast were you going?'

'Not fast. The usual speed.'

Lottie suspected this was still quite fast. She could also tell that Mrs Moore's mind was busy with this information.

'You're a skilled racing driver, Beatrice,' Lottie said. 'How did you manage to accidentally almost hit Hector Johnson as he was walking along the pavement?'

'I don't know! These things just happen. I think I was probably dazzled by the sun.'

'When did this happen?' said Mrs Moore.

'About ten days ago, I think.'

'Then six days ago, Hector Johnson was murdered after a game of poker at which you were present.'

'Now hold on!' responded Beatrice. 'What are you suggesting?'

'I'm suggesting that the man was in danger when he was near you.'

'Two coincidences and nothing more. Are you suggesting that I wished to harm him?'

'I'd like to know for sure. Did you?'

'No! And when I almost hit him with my car, I had no idea who he was.'

Mrs Moore pulled a sceptical face.

'It's the truth!' protested Beatrice. 'What else can I say? Monaco's a small place like everyone says. It's quite easy to bump into someone on more than one occasion.'

'Did you speak to him after you almost killed him?'

'I didn't almost kill him. And yes, I did speak to him and made sure he was alright.'

'He couldn't have been terribly pleased when he discovered he was playing poker with you.'

'I don't think he was bothered either way.'

'Did he mention the incident to you?'

'He did, and we both laughed it off. It became a joke between us.'

'I see.' Mrs Moore seemed unconvinced, and Lottie felt extremely pleased that her employer had done the difficult questioning.

'Well.' Beatrice looked at her watch. 'I'd better be off. Things to do and people to see. I shall catch you around.'

Lottie and Mrs Moore watched her depart.

'Oh dear,' said Mrs Moore. 'I think I've frightened her off. Do you think I was too hard on her, Lottie?'

'No, I don't think you were too hard on her at all. You were incredulous that a driver of her skill could have an accident like that. And to discover the person she almost hit was Hector Johnson is quite revealing.'

'It is, isn't it? Oh, I hope she's as innocent as she claims, Lottie. I've grown to quite like the woman, I couldn't bear it if she turns out to be a murderer!'

'We can't ignore the fact that she went out for a drive this morning at the same time as Michel Rossi.'

'Oh don't! Do you really think she had something to do with his accident?'

'Perhaps she wanted to have her revenge for the manner in which he chased us the other day. Or perhaps it was something more than that? Perhaps she murdered Mr Johnson and Mr Rossi knew it,' said Lottie.

'So she drove him off the road? Oh, how dreadful! Do you really think Beatrice could do such a thing?'

'I don't like to think she can, but the circumstances suggest it at the moment.'

'But why would she drive her car at Hector Johnson? And then murder him in the casino?'

'I don't know. And if she did do it, then it doesn't look like she'd be willing to tell us a motive any time soon.'

'No, it doesn't. I think we've lost ourselves a friend, Lottie.'

'She's not much of a friend if she's a murderer.'

'That's true. You do realise that if you're right about this, then you'll need to tell the commissaire?'

'Yes. But we need more evidence first. I was hoping Beatrice could give us a better explanation, but she didn't, did she? I don't believe her collision with the wall was an accident.'

'Oh look, isn't that Miss Harrison?' said Mrs Moore.

Lottie turned to see the young woman in the lounge, looking about as if trying to find someone.

'Yes, it is. I wonder what she's doing here?'

Chapter Thirty-Four

GRACE HARRISON SEEMED relieved when she caught sight of Lottie and Mrs Moore. She walked over to them.

'I've just heard the news about Michel,' she said. 'I had to speak to someone about it. What a terrible shock! I only saw him a few hours ago.'

'Really?' said Mrs Moore.

'Yes, we had a drink at the Cafe de Paris.'

'Did you know him well?'

'Not very well, no. But we'd had a few discussions about who we thought could have been responsible for Hector Johnson's murder.'

'And who did you come up with?'

'We didn't know! Obviously, we discussed Madame and Monsieur Rochefort, but he didn't like to consider them because he was friendly with them. So the only other one we could come up with was Beatrice.'

'You think she murdered Hector Johnson?'

'Only because we couldn't think who else! I know it sounds silly and we couldn't think of a motive. But we decided that perhaps she had a disagreement with Hector Johnson which we weren't aware of. Or maybe she was just annoyed because he won the poker game.'

'I think that's unlikely,' said Mrs Moore. 'Beatrice seems an experienced gambler to me. I'd be surprised if she suddenly decided to murder someone just because she lost some money.'

'Then perhaps it's something we don't know about,' said Grace. 'Michel and I were discussing whether we should tell the police about Beatrice.'

'Do you have any evidence to suggest it was her?' said Mrs Moore.

'No. But we ruled everyone else out.'

'It could have been one of the Rocheforts,' said Lottie.

'Michel didn't believe it could have been them. He liked them and they lent him their car.'

'I suppose that's one way to keep someone on your side!' chuckled Mrs Moore. 'And besides, poor Michel isn't here anymore. So do you honestly think the Rocheforts are both completely innocent?'

'I think so! Oh, I don't know. I suppose Michel persuaded me they were. I can't believe he's gone! I don't even understand how the accident happened.'

'He was driving dangerously?'

'I know he liked to drive fast. But was it dangerous? I don't know.'

Lottie noticed Beatrice marching towards them, a stern look on her face. She picked up Rosie and cuddled her on her lap, worried what Beatrice was going to say to them now.

'Oh hello, Beatrice,' said Mrs Moore with a note of caution in her voice.

'Hello.' She stood in front of them. 'And hello, Grace. I've come to apologise for my grumpiness earlier. And I'm afraid I wasn't entirely honest with you.'

'Oh?'

Beatrice slumped into a chair. 'I need a gin and lime.'

'Very well.' Mrs Moore called over the waiter and ordered drinks for all four of them.

Beatrice seemed reluctant to speak until she had a drink in her hand, so Mrs Moore made conversation. 'Miss Harrison was just telling us she had a drink with Michel shortly before he had his accident.'

'Really?' said Beatrice. 'How much did he have to drink?'

'Just a couple of glasses of wine,' replied Grace.

'Oh. Because if he'd had a lot, then it would have impaired his judgement and possibly caused the accident. But just a couple of drinks probably wouldn't do much.'

'Really?' said Lottie, not quite believing this.

'Yes. Well I know it doesn't affect me, anyway. I suppose he wasn't as good at driving as he thought he was. Oh, here comes my gin! Lovely.'

The waiter set the drinks on the table and Beatrice grabbed hers and took a gulp.

'So what were you planning to tell us, Beatrice?' asked Mrs Moore.

'Oh yes, that. I actually knew Hector Johnson a little better than I claimed to.'

'Really? How?'

'I spent a few years motor racing in America and I happened to encounter him at Narragansett Park last year. It's a racing track in Rhode Island. It was originally built for horses but automobiles are raced there these days. Hector Johnson, as a wealthy local businessman, was sponsoring the event. I participated in the time trials and was the fastest person there that day. And when it was time for Hector Johnson to present the trophy, do you know what he did?'

'What?'

'Refused to give it to me because I'm a woman.'

'No!'

'The American Automobile Association banned women from motor racing in 1909.'

'What?'

'But this wasn't an AAA affiliated event, it was just a bit of fun and, instead, Mr Johnson said I shouldn't have been racing and gave the trophy to the chap who came second. I can't remember his name now.'

'But that's terrible!'

'So you can understand my anger when I saw Hector Johnson strolling along that path without a care in the world. I'd come to Monaco for a bit of fun and there he was! It was a rash act and I realise now I could have killed him. But I was gripped by such anger that the steering wheel pretty much steered the car directly at him. I slowed down a little bit because I didn't want to go through the wall and over the clifftop. And I only wanted to shake him up a little bit, it wasn't an attempt on his life. I merely wanted him to reflect on his actions. With hindsight, I suppose I was going fast enough to have caused him serious injury if he hadn't leapt out of the way. That man had quick reactions.'

'But not quick enough to save him from the second attempt on his life.'

'No. He succumbed to that one, didn't he? I'm not sorry he's gone. But I didn't do it, if that's what you've been thinking.'

Chapter Thirty-Five

AFTER HEARING BEATRICE'S EXPLANATION, Lottie felt the need for another walk. She took Rosie to the casino terraces which were bathed in the golden sunshine of late afternoon.

Was Beatrice's explanation plausible? She had admitted now how she'd really felt about Hector Johnson. Presumably she'd kept quiet on the matter out of worry she'd be accused of murder. Was she telling the truth?

'Oh!' The dramatic sigh came from a woman in sapphire blue who'd just sunk onto a nearby bench with her head in her hands.

Rosie trotted over to her and the lady raised her head.

'Madame Rochefort?' said Lottie, stepping over to her. 'Are you alright?'

'No!' the woman wailed in reply. 'I am distraught!' Her eyes were red and her face was pale.

'Why?'

'Because I think my husband might be a murderer!'

'Really?'

'Yes! I know it sounds terrible, doesn't it? But the more I think about it, the more I realise it must be him.'

Could Madame Rochefort be right? Lottie wasn't sure. 'What makes you think it was him?'

'He had plenty of reasons to murder Hector.'

'Such as what?'

'He'd invited Hector to join one of Philippe Albertini's criminal schemes. You probably don't know who Albertini is, he's a criminal from Marseille. Joseph had been trying to persuade Hector to invest some money into Albertini's scheme, and Hector refused. I think my husband must have realised there was a risk Hector would tell people what my husband and Albertini were up to. That's why he murdered him!'

It seemed a plausible reason to Lottie. 'How would your husband have gone about it that evening?' she asked.

'I don't know. I suppose he must have taken Hector's reading glasses and hidden them so Hector had to return to the room to fetch them. And he must have hidden behind the curtain and attacked Hector once he was in the room!'

'Where were you during this time?'

'Me?' She seemed baffled by the question, then recovered herself. 'I was playing roulette.'

'Did you wonder where your husband was?'

'No. I just assumed he was at another table or discussing business with someone somewhere.'

'And how was your husband when you saw him again?' Lottie imagined his demeanour must have been a little different if he'd just strangled someone with a curtain rope.

'He was his normal self. But that's my husband for you.'

'Has he ever attacked someone before?'

'Not that I know of, but he could well have done.'

'What makes you so sure?'

Madame Rochefort scowled a little, as if annoyed by

Lottie's questioning. Perhaps she hadn't expected this level of scrutiny. 'Because I know my husband,' she snapped.

'Have you told the police?'

'Well, I suggested to the commissaire that my husband was capable of such an act, but he appeared to be falling asleep while I was speaking to him. It's completely hopeless. I don't think anybody's interested in how I feel.'

'I am.'

She gave a faint smile. 'Well, that's kind of you, Miss Sprigg. It's extremely upsetting when you come to realise the ugly truth about someone you love.'

'If you really think your husband committed the murder, Madame Rochefort, then you should try speaking to the police again.'

'I know.' She dabbed at her eyes. 'I shall try it. But I may need someone else to convince them too.' The look she gave Lottie left her in no doubt who she meant.

Lottie didn't know what to say. She wasn't convinced that Joseph Rochefort was any more guilty than the other people in the room that evening. And what if this conversation with Madame Rochefort was merely a ruse of hers to cover up her own guilt?

The Frenchwoman's expression grew a little steelier, as if she wasn't completely happy with Lottie's reaction. 'Perhaps you need some time to think about it,' she said, getting to her feet. 'You do realise that my husband thinks you're working undercover for the French police?'

Lottie couldn't resist a laugh. 'Really? Why?'

'He thinks you're watching him. The manner in which you suddenly turned up at our hotel made him suspicious.'

'I realise now that was a mistake.'

'It made him paranoid, and that's why he sent Michel after you.'

'After me?'

'Yes. I believe you encountered him on a mountain road. Joseph asked him to frighten you off. But he was unable to. You're a very brave girl, Miss Sprigg. It wasn't nice of Michel and it wasn't nice of my husband either. I think he needs to be dealt with before he can cause any more harm. Have a think about how you can help me with that, Miss Sprigg.'

Chapter Thirty-Six

MRS MOORE WAS ONLY HALFWAY through her breakfast the following morning when a waiter informed her that Prince Manfred's car was waiting for her outside.

'Good golly, I do wish he'd give me more notice with these things,' she said to Lottie. 'He's clearly an early riser. What time is it?'

'Half-past nine.'

'Too early.'

As messages were passed between the car, the waiting staff, and Mrs Moore, it was established that Prince Manfred wished to take Mrs Moore for a day trip to Nice.

'But that's in France, isn't it?' she said to the waiter. 'How long does it take to get there?'

'About half an hour in a car.'

'Oh. I thought it would be longer.' She turned to Lottie. 'Do you mind if I spend the day with the prince, Lottie?'

'Not at all. Isn't that the reason we're here in Monaco?'

'Oh yes! I suppose it is.' She laughed. 'Well, I'd better get ready. What a shame I don't have time to finish my boiled egg.'

. . .

Lottie helped Mrs Moore ready herself, then waved her off in Prince Manfred's car from the hotel steps. She was just about to return to the lobby when a police car parked in the gap left by the prince's vehicle. A policeman and a short, wide, bespectacled man with a grey moustache got out. It was Commissaire Verrando.

'Just the lady I'm here to see,' he said, as he climbed the hotel steps. 'We need your help.'

'How?'

'We need to speak with Miss Grace Harrison, I understand you're a friend of hers?'

'Sort of. I don't know her very well, but I'm friendly with her.'

Lottie recalled that he had seen her talking to Grace the previous day.

'Please may you come with us?' he said.

'Why?'

'We need to go to her hotel and speak with her, but we need you with us.'

'I don't understand.'

'She will want to see a friendly face. Not my face!' He laughed. 'We need you to visit her at her hotel and chat to her about something. Then we'll turn up.'

'So you want me to pretend it's a social visit?'

'Yes.'

'But that would mean lying.'

'Yes, it would, but we have several reports that Miss Harrison has committed a few crimes, so you're not doing a bad thing.'

'What reason can I give her for turning up at her hotel?'

'Perhaps you'd like to ask her to join you for a walk? I saw the pair of you walking together yesterday.'

Lottie considered the request. She wasn't keen to do it,

but Grace had admitted to stealing from people. It looked like her crimes were about to catch up with her.

Reluctantly, Lottie agreed and told the commissaire she would be ready to join him in ten minutes. 'Can my dog come too?' she asked.

'Of course.'

A SHORT WHILE LATER, Lottie and Rosie climbed out of the police car outside a modest building called the Hôtel Riviera.

'What do you need me to do?' she asked Commissaire Verrando.

'Knock on her door and ask her to join you for a walk. We will meet you both down here in the lobby.'

'Do you really need me to do it? Can't you go up to her room?'

'We could, but there's a danger she gets upset about seeing me and my colleague. The room has a balcony and what if she runs out onto there and... well, you get the idea. We need her in a place where we can safely detain her. That would be the best option for us. If it doesn't work, then we'll have to go into her room, but we prefer not to do that.'

Lottie sighed.

'It's very important that we speak to her about the stolen money,' continued the commissaire. 'I know you like Miss Harrison, but if she's been stealing from people, then she needs to be arrested.'

Lottie nodded. She felt sure Grace would view her actions as a betrayal, but this seemed the right thing to do.

They stepped into the small lobby and the commissaire exchanged a nod with the red-haired lady behind the reception desk, as if they'd already agreed the plan.

'She's in room twelve,' said the commissaire. 'We'll wait

here in the lobby. Just encourage her to come downstairs if you can.'

Lottie and Rosie climbed the narrow staircase to Grace's room on the first floor. She felt guilty about calling on Grace under false pretences.

She found room twelve and paused for a moment before knocking on the door. She looked down at Rosie and the corgi returned her glance with her large dark eyes.

Lottie knocked at the door and her heart thudded as she waited for an answer. She tried to calm herself and put a smile on her face. What was Grace going to say when she realised she'd been tricked?

There was no answer, so Lottie knocked again. She grew hopeful that Grace wasn't in the room. With a bit of luck, she was out and Lottie could have no further involvement.

After knocking again and waiting a little longer, Lottie decided there was little more she could do. 'Come on, Rosie,' she whispered. 'Let's tell them she's not here.'

She went back downstairs to where the commissaire and the police officer waited. 'I don't think she's there,' she said.

'Strange,' said Commissaire Verrando. He addressed the red-haired receptionist. 'Are you sure Miss Harrison is in her room?'

'I haven't seen her go out today.'

'But can you be sure she hasn't gone out?'

'No.'

He groaned and ordered the policeman to fetch a room key from the receptionist. 'Let's look at the room,' he said. 'Please can you come with us, Miss Sprigg?'

'Must I?'

'She may be there. Perhaps she's asleep? We'd like you with us just so she doesn't become too worried.'

'Alright then.'

Reluctantly, Lottie accompanied them back up the stairs.

She waited and held her breath as the policeman unlocked the door and slowly opened it. He peered inside, then turned to the commissaire. 'All clear.'

They stepped into the room, it was small and untidy.

The policeman opened drawers and the wardrobe.

'What are you looking for?' asked Lottie.

'Anything suspicious,' said the commissaire. 'Something which could have been stolen. Money or other valuables.'

The policeman dropped to his knees and peered under the bed. Then he lifted the mattress and looked under there too.

Lottie noticed the wastepaper bin was filled with ripped up pieces of paper. Had Grace been destroying something? More papers lay on the dressing table. Lottie looked through them in an effort to help. There seemed to be little of interest until she came across a folded piece of paper. She unfolded it and saw it looked remarkably familiar. It was a note written on headed paper from the Hôtel Hermitage Monte-Carlo.

I warned you but you didn't listen, now you're for it.

It was exactly the same as the note which had been sent to Hector Johnson. Except this note didn't have an error in it. So it wasn't the same note, but it said the same thing.

Someone had threatened both Grace and Hector.

But who?

'Have you found something?' asked the commissaire.

'No.' She folded up the note and replaced it. 'Nothing.'

She decided not to tell the commissaire about it until she'd worked out what it meant.

Chapter Thirty-Seven

LOTTIE RESTED in her room when she returned to the Hôtel de Paris with Rosie. She picked up her book of detective stories, then put it down again. Her mind was too busy to read.

She thought of the two notes on the headed notepaper from the Hôtel Hermitage. Had Joseph Rochefort written them? His wife seemed convinced he was the murderer and his motive seemed strong. It made sense that he'd wanted to stop Hector Johnson from telling people about his criminal activities. And although he was French, he'd presumably written the notes in English because that was the language both Grace and Hector spoke. Lottie could understand now why he'd threatened Hector. But why had he threatened Grace? Had she stolen from him, too?

And although Marie Rochefort had sounded convincing, how could Lottie be sure she was telling the truth? If Marie had murdered Hector Johnson, then she could be blaming her husband to cover up her own guilt. The manner in which she'd confided in Lottie the previous evening had seemed strange. She'd appeared out of nowhere and made a show of her upset. And hadn't she requested Lottie's help? It seemed too odd to be genuine.

And then there was Beatrice. She'd almost killed Hector Johnson once. Had she tried a second time?

And where was Grace? Did she know who'd sent her the note?

'I've got an idea,' Lottie said to Rosie. 'Let's go to the Hôtel Hermitage. After that, we'll go and find Commissaire Verrando. And after that, we'll wait for Mrs Moore to return from her trip to Nice.'

Chapter Thirty-Eight

'We had a lovely day, Lottie,' said Mrs Moore. 'We strolled along the seafront and had lunch at the most wonderful seafood restaurant. And Boris was such fun! He really is good company.'

'And the prince?'

'He was wonderful fun, too. The three of us thoroughly enjoyed ourselves. Now, where are you taking me, Lottie?'

'To the police station.'

'Why?'

'I've spoken to Commissaire Verrando, and he's agreed to invite everyone there this evening.'

'Everyone?'

'Everyone who could have had something to do with Hector Johnson's death. Although Grace is already there because she was arrested earlier today.'

'For what?'

'Stealing money, apparently.'

'Golly! Young Grace? She doesn't look like she'd do something like that. What a surprise. And how did you persuade the commissaire to invite everyone else?'

'I shared a theory with him and he thought it sounded interesting.'

'What theory? You must tell me, Lottie!'

'I'll tell you what I can on the way there.'

Lottie looked down at Rosie and smiled. She'd already explained everything to her pet, but the corgi's lips were sealed.

A SHORT WHILE LATER, Lottie, Mrs Moore and Rosie sat in Commissaire Verrando's office with Beatrice and Grace.

'Well this is cosy, isn't it?' said Beatrice.

Grace gave them a sullen greeting. A policeman stood by her chair, presumably guarding her.

Marie and Joseph Rochefort were the last to arrive. 'Isn't there a better chair than this one?' protested Joseph.

'You'd have got a better chair if you'd arrived on time,' said the commissaire, surveying him from his superior seat. The Rocheforts sat down and the commissaire turned to Lottie. 'Which language shall we speak in?' he asked.

'English,' said Lottie. 'If that's alright?'

'I think everyone here has a basic grasp of it, so that should be fine.' He raised his voice to address the room. 'I've invited you all here because this young lady thinks each of you had a motive for murdering Hector Johnson.'

'Such as what?' said Joseph Rochefort.

Lottie took in a breath and tried to remain calm and confident. 'Your wife told me your motive,' she said.

'What?' He turned to Marie Rochefort. 'You did what?'

Marie Rochefort pursed her lips.

'What have you been saying about me?' demanded her husband.

'Your wife told me you invited Hector Johnson to invest in a criminal scheme which Philippe Albertini was planning,' said Lottie.

'Who's Philippe Albertini?' asked Mrs Moore.

'An unpleasant gentleman from Marseille who bribes, blackmails, racketeers and smuggles opium from Turkey,' said Madame Rochefort.

'Good gracious!'

'Sadly, that's the sort of company my husband likes to keep and, understandably, Hector didn't wish to be involved with such a man.'

'You introduced the American businessman to the French criminal?' asked Mrs Moore.

'He did,' said Madame Rochefort. 'And it didn't go well. I suspect my husband was worried Hector would tell the authorities about the deal. He couldn't risk that happening.'

'So he murdered him?' asked Beatrice.

'I believe so.'

'What nonsense!' spat Monsieur Rochefort. 'I will admit to you all now that I have discussed business with Philippe Albertini, knowing that he is a criminal. I was under no illusion about his activities. And although it was only a discussion, I fully expect there will be an investigation into my conduct and, sadly, perhaps that will affect my family business in Paris. Perhaps the store will even be closed down. Who knows? It makes me sad to think of it, but I suppose it will be the price I have to pay for associating myself with someone like Albertini. But murder? I could never do such a thing! I may be many things, but I am not a murderer!'

'Even though you ordered Michel Rossi to drive Miss Sprigg off the road?' said his wife.

'I didn't order him to do such a thing! His instructions were merely to give her a fright and warn her off. I thought she'd been employed by the French police to spy on me!'

'Even though you asked Michel to only frighten Lottie,' said Beatrice. 'It was still a very dangerous thing to do.'

'I realise that now. And I regret it. I was panicking. I didn't want to get found out.' He turned to his wife. 'And what a betrayal from a woman I once loved. I notice you haven't admitted your love affair with Hector.'

Marie Rochefort's face coloured.

He addressed everyone else. 'It began when he paid us a visit in Paris. My wife thought I wouldn't notice, but I did.'

'So why did you wish to do business with him afterwards?' asked his wife.

'Because the man had a lot of money. And he was a fool! He was just the person Albertini and I needed. We needed someone with a lot of money and who would lose his investment.'

'So you were planning to swindle Hector Johnson?' asked Mrs Moore.

'Albertini was. I was merely making the introduction. If you're looking for the murderer, then you really need to look no further than my wife!'

'Interesting,' said Commissaire Verrando. 'Madame Rochefort's cigarette case was found at the scene of the crime.'

'Because I'd lent it to Hector!' said Marie Rochefort. 'He must have had it in his hand at the time.'

'Monsieur Rochefort, I'm interested to know why you think your wife murdered Mr Johnson,' said Beatrice.

'I suspect it was because he was going to reveal their affair. She couldn't bear the shame of it.'

'Is this true?' Beatrice asked Madame Rochefort.

'Possibly.'

'Was he threatening to tell your husband about your affair?'

'He wanted me to divorce my husband and marry him. He got quite insistent about it.'

'But all along I knew about them, anyway!' Monsieur Rochefort laughed. 'Ridiculous, isn't it? Marie was so worried about me finding out something I already knew that she murdered him. What a waste!'

'I didn't murder him!' protested his wife. 'And if you must know, I did plan to marry him! I was working with the French police to have you arrested. And, once that had been done, I was going to begin a new life with Hector.'

'There you have it!' He pointed at his wife. 'Surely there is no greater betrayal?'

'It's certainly betrayal,' said Mrs Moore. 'But I don't see why your wife would murder someone she was planning to spend the rest of her days with.'

'It's just more lies to cover her tracks. She wanted me out of the way. She probably regrets that she didn't murder me instead of him!'

'I didn't murder him!' she protested.

Mrs Moore sighed, as if growing weary of the bickering. 'If you ask me,' she said. 'The most likely person to have murdered Hector Johnson is the person who tried once before.'

Beatrice gasped. 'Surely you can't mean me, Roberta?'

'You drove your car at him.'

'Is that so?' said Monsieur Rochefort. 'I didn't know about that!'

'I never intended to hit him, it was just something to...'

'Frighten him?' suggested Joseph Rochefort.

'Yes.'

'Well, if you ask me, it's all quite absurd,' said Mrs Moore. 'Lots of people going about frightening others but never actually claiming responsibility for the murder of Mr Johnson.'

'Perhaps I should start at the beginning,' said Lottie. 'As most of you know, I found Hector Johnson's jacket under a bench on the casino terrace. I found a note in his pocket. It said, "I warned you but you didn't listen, now you're for it."

But "your" was crossed out because it had been misspelled and the word "you're" was written next to it.'

'It sounds the same,' said Beatrice.

'Yes, it does. But it's different when written down.'

'The English language is so confusing.'

Lottie continued, 'Earlier today, I discovered a similar note in Grace Harrison's room and it said the same, except there was no error in it. Both notes were written on headed paper from the Hôtel Hermitage which suggested to me that the person who wrote them was staying there.'

'Two threatening notes?' said Beatrice. 'One sent to Hector and one sent to Grace?'

'Yes. I made some enquiries at the Hôtel Hermitage and discovered Mr Johnson stayed there, but none of the other suspects did.'

'Suspects?' said Monsieur Rochefort.

'She means us,' said his wife.

'I'd always assumed that Hector Johnson's murderer had written that note,' said Lottie. 'But then I had another thought. What if he wrote it himself?'

Joseph Rochefort laughed. 'Why would he write a threatening note to himself?'

'He didn't write it to himself,' said Lottie. 'It wasn't addressed to anyone, so we don't actually know who the note was for. It was only when I saw the similar note in Grace Harrison's room that I suspected the note had been written for her.'

'So why were there two notes?' asked Beatrice.

'Because he made a mistake in the first one,' said Lottie. 'And he decided to rewrite it.'

'And put the first one in his jacket pocket?'

'Presumably because he didn't want anyone else to find it.'

'Why not destroy it?'

'I don't know. Perhaps he didn't have time when he wrote

the notes, but was planning to destroy it when he had the chance.'

'But what's the evidence that Hector Johnson wrote that note?' asked Beatrice. 'It could have been someone else who sent the notes to both Hector and Grace.'

'The only evidence is that the notes were written on headed paper from the hotel he was staying at,' said Lottie. 'I don't know what his handwriting was like. But it's a question which could be put to Miss Harrison.'

Miss Harrison shuffled uncomfortably.

'Do you know who sent you that note, Grace?' asked Beatrice.

The young woman gave a slight nod.

'How did you know it was from Hector Johnson?'

'Because it repeated what he'd told me in person.'

'Was it his handwriting?'

'I don't know. But I assumed it was from him.'

'Why did he write it?' asked Joseph Rochefort.

'Because I stole money from him.'

'You stole from him and murdered him?'

'No, I only stole.'

'She stole from several people,' added the commissaire. 'That's why she was arrested earlier today.'

'And she murdered Hector Johnson too,' said Lottie.

'Really?' said Beatrice. 'Grace?'

The young woman said nothing.

'Just a minute,' said Monsieur Rochefort. 'How do you know it was Grace Harrison who murdered Hector Johnson, Miss Sprigg? There's no more evidence against her than there is against the rest of us.'

'You're right,' said Lottie. 'But Grace said something the other day which stuck in my mind. We met on a boat trip organised by Prince Manfred of Bavaria and discussed the murder. During that conversation, Grace said she was surprised no one at the tables outside the Cafe de Paris saw the murderer through the window while they were hiding behind the curtain. And that made me wonder, how did she know what the view from the window was?'

'She looked out of it?' suggested Beatrice.

'When? From what I understand, on the evening of Mr Johnson's murder, the curtains were drawn throughout the entire poker game, isn't that right?'

Joseph Rochefort gave this some thought. 'Yes, you're right.'

'So someone could only know what the view from the window was if they opened the curtains in that room. Did anyone open the curtains during the game?'

'No.' The others shook their heads.

'But someone hiding behind the curtain would have seen the view,' said Mrs Moore.

'Yes.'

Beatrice gasped. 'Grace! Was it really you?'

The young woman slumped forward in her chair, her face in her hands.

Chapter Thirty-Nine

'I DIDN'T MEAN to do it!' wailed Grace.

'You meant to frighten him?' suggested Mrs Moore with a wry smile.

'I did it to protect myself,' said Grace. 'You've heard about the note he sent me. He was going to kill me!'

'He merely said you were "for it",' said Marie Rochefort. 'That doesn't suggest he was going to murder you.'

'But I was scared he was going to!'

'So you stole from him and then panicked when he confronted you about it?' said Marie Rochefort.

'Yes. I stole the money from his wallet when we had dinner one evening. It's how I made a living and I'm not proud of myself. I'm not going to do it anymore. Anyway, he confronted me about it the following day and I denied it. He was furious and asked for the money, but I couldn't repay him because I'd already used it to pay off my overdue hotel bill. And then he confronted me again the following day and told me I would be dealt with. I took that to be a threat and then I received the note. It was pushed under my hotel room door.'

'Why didn't he just report you to the police?' said Mrs Moore.

'I don't know.'

'Perhaps he didn't want any involvement with the police because he was in Monaco to discuss investing money with a criminal,' said Marie Rochefort. 'But you deserved to receive that note, Grace, you were a silly girl stealing from him like that.'

'I regret it now.'

'More than you regret the murder?' said Joseph Rochefort.

'I regret that too! But I only did to him what I felt sure he was going to do to me.'

'You must be stronger than you look to overpower someone like that,' said Mrs Moore.

'I am. But it's also because I attacked him when he wasn't expecting it. He had no idea I was there when he returned to the poker room.

'The plan formed in my mind after I received that note from him. I'd already played poker in those private rooms and I knew the curtains were always drawn for privacy. I also knew the curtains were large and heavy enough for someone to hide behind.

'He wasn't happy to see me at that poker game and he didn't want me to be there. That's why we had a brief argument before we went into the room. I challenged him to beat me and told him he'd probably feel a lot better once he'd won some money off me.'

'So it was you who took his reading glasses?' said Beatrice.

'Yes. He was taking them on and off during the game and, when we'd finished, he rested them on the table. I managed to knock them off the table with no one noticing.'

'But how?' said Lottie. 'You weren't even sitting next to him.'

'It was once the game had finished and everyone was getting up from their seats at the time. I asked Beatrice for a cigarette and I pushed the glasses off the table then.'

'I didn't even notice that,' said Beatrice.

'Then, a few minutes later, I pretended to drop my bag,' said Grace. 'And that's when I went under the table to retrieve it and take the glasses.'

'Quite clever,' said Monsieur Rochefort. 'Because if someone had seen you knock the reading glasses onto the floor, you could just have claimed it was an accident.'

'So you pocketed the reading glasses,' said Mrs Moore. 'And everyone left the room.'

'I put them in my handbag,' said Grace. 'And left the room with everyone else. Once I was sure Michel had left the room, I returned and put the glasses on the table and hid behind the curtain. I'd seen the rope ties on other curtains in the casino and I remember thinking what a useful weapon they would be.'

'Really?'

'I suppose that's how my mind works. I see a rope and I have dark thoughts about it. I waited for a few minutes and, as planned, Hector returned to the room. I heard him say something like "There they are" when he saw the glasses. I had the curtain rope in my hand and I peered out from behind the curtain at just the right time. He had his back to me and was about to leave the room. That's when I pounced.'

Lottie gave a shudder.

'I wish now I hadn't done it. It was foolish and rash, but I was frightened and I didn't know what else to do!' Grace wiped her eyes. 'Strangely, I feel better being honest about this. It's awful having to keep such secrets to yourself. Always watching your back and worrying that someone's going to catch up with you. It's a horrible way to live.'

'I can imagine it is,' said Mrs Moore.

'So I suppose, while everyone is listening, I should also confess to the murder of Michel Rossi.'

'*What*?' said Beatrice. 'But that was an accident, wasn't it?'

'Yes, it was. But only because I put sleeping tablets into his glass of wine.'

'Oh good golly,' said Mrs Moore, her hand on her chest. 'What a thing to do!'

'I think he suspected me of Hector's murder all along. He kept asking me questions about that evening. He asked me if I had taken Hector's reading glasses and he kept asking me to account for my whereabouts after the poker game had finished. That's when I was hiding behind the curtain, of course, so I had no alibi. I grew tired of it and I knew he enjoyed driving Madame and Monsieur Rochefort's car every day. So I invited him to have a lunchtime drink with me, pretending I was going to tell him everything he wanted to hear. And that's when I put the sleeping tablets into his wine. They were tablets which had been prescribed to me and I ground them up into a powder and ensured he had a couple of glasses of red wine.'

'And he didn't notice?'

'By the time he drank the second one, he commented there was something in it, but I think he decided it was sediment from the bottom of the bottle.'

'So Michel Rossi drove off up the mountain, having consumed a large dose of sleeping tablets,' said Beatrice. 'No wonder he couldn't negotiate a bend in the road!'

'The wine must have had an effect too,' said Mrs Moore. 'Quite unbelievable.'

Lottie recalled how Grace had sought out her and Mrs Moore after hearing the news of Michel's death, pretending to be upset. She struggled to look at her now, she was duplicitous and cruel.

The commissaire spoke next, 'A full confession. Just what

we like to hear. If no one has anything else to add, then Miss Harrison will be taken to the cells now.'

A knock sounded at the door.

'Come in!' said the commissaire.

The door opened and two men stepped into the room. Then they both retreated a little, taken aback by the number of people in the room.

'My apologies for the interruption,' said the older of the two. 'I am Detective Brunelle of the Marseille Police. I'm here to arrest Monsieur Joseph Rochefort.'

'Me?' said Joseph Rochefort. 'What have I done?'

'Conspired to invest money in a racketeering scheme.'

Lottie noticed a smile on Marie Rochefort's face.

'Do you mind if we arrest him, Commissaire Verrando?' asked Detective Brunelle.

'Go ahead. You're French and he's French, I'll let you deal with him over the border in France.'

'Very well.' He pulled out some handcuffs.

'What about Philippe Albertini?' asked the commissaire. 'Have you got him?'

'Yes, he's sitting in the back of the police van as we speak.'

'Well done.'

Detective Brunelle turned to Marie Rochefort. 'Your husband will be held in Marseille police station if you would like to visit him tomorrow.'

'Thank you,' said Marie. 'I might drop in if I have time.'

Chapter Forty

'HOPEFULLY I'LL HAVE time to finish my boiled egg this morning,' said Mrs Moore at breakfast the following day. 'Prince Manfred is off on a fishing trip today, but may call on me later. Oh, I completely forgot to tell you, Lottie. He's off to Vienna tomorrow.'

'Vienna? So does that mean...'

'That we're going there too? Yes, of course!'

'Well, it will be nice to see Vienna. Although I'm going to miss being by the sea.'

'Me too. And I'm hoping our stay there will be a little less eventful. We've been kept rather busy recently, haven't we? It's quite exhausting. Well done with solving Hector Johnson's case, though. Once again, you did some remarkable work, Lottie. I never would have suspected that young Grace woman. What a terrible mess she's made of her life! A cautionary tale for anyone thinking of doing something similar. You can't just go about the place stealing from people, can you? You'll always get your comeuppance one way or the other.'

Beatrice approached their table, wearing her motoring

overalls. 'It's a beautiful day, isn't it?' She peered out at the sunshine beyond the window. 'And I've just realised that you haven't come out for a spin with me yet, Roberta.'

'Me?'

'Yes. Who else do you think I'm talking to?'

'What does a spin involve, exactly?'

'A little drive on the mountain roads. Come on Roberta, you'll love it. Feel the wind on your face and the thrilling sense of freedom!'

'Unfortunately, I have some other plans today, Beatrice.'

'That's a shame. Tomorrow?'

'Oh yes. Tomorrow.'

'I'll see you then.'

Mrs Moore watched Beatrice walk away, then lowered her voice. 'Don't tell her we're going to Vienna tomorrow, Lottie. Not yet, anyway.'

A waiter approached their table and addressed Lottie.

'You have a visitor in reception, Miss Sprigg.'

'Oh, thank you.'

'I wonder who that is?' said Mrs Moore. 'Go and see.'

Lottie did so, taking Rosie with her. She smiled when she saw her visitor was Henri.

'I'm sorry to interrupt you,' he said. 'But I thought you might like to know that Commissaire Verrando has arrested the young Englishwoman, Grace Harrison, for the murder of Hector Johnson and Michel Rossi. Can you believe she murdered Michel, too? She put sleeping tablets in his wine and that caused the crash. Oh...' He watched her face for a moment. 'You don't seem surprised. You've heard already?'

'Yes. In fact, I suggested to Commissaire Verrando that Grace Harrison was the culprit.'

'Really? How did you work that out?'

'It's quite complicated. But I can explain it to you if you'd like to join me for a walk with Rosie?'

'I'd love to!' He beamed. 'But you do realise that Commissaire Verrando is taking all the credit for solving the case? He hasn't mentioned that you helped him at all!'

'Oh well, perhaps this will be his last case before he retires. And let's not forget that you helped me. I couldn't have managed it without you. Thank you.'

'That's alright, I didn't do much. But I'd be furious about Commissaire Verrando if I were you!'

'There's little point in being furious, what does it solve? And besides, I won't be in Monaco for much longer, my employer and I are departing tomorrow.'

Henri's face fell. 'Where to?'

'Vienna.'

'Oh? Well, I've heard it's nice there.' He rubbed his brow. 'It's a shame you're leaving.'

'But that's tomorrow. We still have today.'

'Yes. We do.' He smiled.

'I'll meet you for a walk with Rosie in half an hour.'

THE END

Thank you

Thank you for reading this Lottie Sprigg mystery. I really hope you enjoyed it! Here are a few ways to stay in touch:

- Join my mailing list and receive a FREE short story *Murder in Milan*: marthabond.com/murder-in-milan
- Like my brand new Facebook page: facebook.com/marthabondauthor

Murder in Vienna

Book 5 in the Lottie Sprigg Mystery Series.

A Viennese victim and a puzzle at the palace!

Lottie Sprigg and her employer, Mrs Moore, are guests at Vienna's opulent Schönbrunn Palace. But their visit goes awry when the corpse of a renowned psychoanalyst is found in the grounds. There's a handful of suspects and - tragically for Mrs Moore - one of them is her beloved Prince Manfred.

Mrs Moore is devastated that her beau has been caught up in the crime. And she soon discovers he's been keeping other secrets from her, too.

Lottie is tasked with proving Prince Manfred's innocence. But with overwhelming evidence against him, has she any chance of success? As she scours Vienna for clues, Lottie wonders if the jolly Bavarian prince has been hiding a darker side all along...

Get your copy: mybook.to/viennamurder

A free Lottie Sprigg mystery

Find out what happens when Lottie, Rosie and Mrs Moore catch the train to Paris in this free mystery *Murder in Milan*!

Lottie and Mrs Moore are travelling from Venice to Paris when their journey is halted at Milan. A passenger has been poisoned and no one can resume their trip until the killer is caught. Trapped in a dismal hotel with her corgi sidekick, Lottie is handed a mysterious suitcase which could land her in trouble...

Events escalate with a second poisoning. Lottie must clear her name and find the killer before the trip is cancelled for good!

Visit my website to claim your free copy:
marthabond.com/murder-in-milan

Or scan the code on the following page:

Also by Martha Bond

Lottie Sprigg Country House Mystery Series:

Murder in the Library
Murder in the Grotto
Murder in the Maze

Writing as Emily Organ:

Augusta Peel Mystery Series:

Death in Soho
Murder in the Air
The Bloomsbury Murder
The Tower Bridge Murder
Death in Westminster

Penny Green Mystery Series:

Limelight
The Rookery

ALSO BY MARTHA BOND

The Maid's Secret
The Inventor
Curse of the Poppy
The Bermondsey Poisoner
An Unwelcome Guest
Death at the Workhouse
The Gang of St Bride's
Murder in Ratcliffe
The Egyptian Mystery
The Camden Spiritualist

Churchill & Pemberley Mystery Series:

Tragedy at Piddleton Hotel
Murder in Cold Mud
Puzzle in Poppleford Wood
Trouble in the Churchyard
Wheels of Peril
The Poisoned Peer
Fiasco at the Jam Factory
Disaster at the Christmas Dinner
Christmas Calamity at the Vicarage (novella)

Printed in Great Britain
by Amazon

38877486R00121